I0714388

THE RETURN OF THE NEANDERTHALS

From the Beginning to Fighting Criminals to Joining a Gang

The First Episodes in Three Books: The Neanderthals Are Back, The Rise of the Force, and The Rise of the Gang

THE RETURN OF THE NEANDERTHALS

Copyright © 2021 by Gini Graham Scott

All rights reserved. No part of this book may be used or reproduced by any means, graphic, electronic, or mechanical, including photocopying, recording, taping or by any information storage retrieval system without the written permission of the author except in the case of brief quotations embodied in critical articles and reviews.

TABLE OF CONTENTS

INTRODUCTION

The story of the Neanderthals is truly fascinating. There are hundreds of sites where their bones have been discovered in Europe and Southern and Central South Asia, and these sites contain more than 300 bodies that date back to about 250,000 to 350,000 years ago. The Neanderthals thrived for hundreds of thousands of years, and, for a time, they appear to have lived separately from Homo sapiens until about 100,000 to 30,000 years ago. Sometime during this period, some Neanderthals interbred with humans, so now modern humans have about 1-4% Neanderthal DNA. Then, suddenly, about 30,000 to 40,000 years ago they went extinct.

Who Are the Neanderthals?

Why did they go extinct? The question seems to fascinate scientists who are still debating the reasons, though they commonly express surprise at the Neanderthals' quick extinction. The irony is that the Neanderthals were especially adapted to the cold spell that hit Europe for thousands of years, while modern humans who moved in from Africa and Southern Asia were not. Yet, modern humans thrived, while Neanderthals died off.

Before their disappearance, though, Neanderthals dominated their territory. They were especially strong, fierce hunters, who hunted all types of game, including the mammoth and woolly rhinoceros. They were skilled at hunting in groups and used ambush hunting to trap their prey. They also had a language and skills to communicate, so they could organize small groups to hunt game, much like wolves hunt in packs to trap and kill their prey.

Mostly they lived in caves in small family groups that combined into small communities of perhaps 10 to 15 families. They had fire, too, and burned it in fire pits. They obtained it from natural events like lightning strikes and forest fires and tended the fire to keep it going. They also could make it by smashing mineral pyrite against flint to create sparks, which they nursed into a large fire.

They appear to have cared for their sick and buried their dead in their caves, and even had the beginnings of symbolic thinking and art in the form of handprints in red ochre found in some caves. They also made jewelry.

There is evidence that they engaged in cannibalism at times, perhaps after succeeding in a battle with another group.

Taking all of that information together, I imagined that the Neanderthals might have had the brain power of a modern five or six year old. Then, I wondered about the possibility of bringing the Neanderthals back, since there have been some recent developments in bringing back once extinct species.

How We Can Bring Back the Neanderthal

Recent developments in extracting DNA from bones using gene editing techniques and cloning show that it will be possible to bring back Neanderthals, since scientists developed some new techniques to bring back several mammals from extinction.

One is the Pyrenean Ibex, the first mammal brought back briefly and there are continuing efforts to bring it back by cloning it from preserved cells, according to an article "Fresh Effort to Clone Extinct Animal" by Paul Rincon in the BBC news.

Likewise, Australian scientists are working on bringing back the extinct thylacine, popularly known as the Tasmanian tiger, because the last known live animal was found in Tasmania in 1933. They have sought to bring it back using a technique developed by Harvard geneticist George Church, according to several news articles. One is by Peter Devlin for the *Daily Mail* in Australia: "'It's Not Science Fiction, It's Science Fact': Australian Scientists Plan to Clone the Tasmanian Tiger and Bring It Back from Extinction." Another article is by John Pickrell explaining the process for Cosmos Magazine: "Return of the Living Thylacine."

Additionally, under the leadership of George Church, scientists have sought to clone the mammoth using the DNA of its closest living relative, the Asian elephant. In California, the Revive and Restore organization is supporting the work of its lead scientist Ben Novak and other "de-extinction" scientists to use genetic engineering and the CRISPR gene editing tool to revive selected extinct animals, such as the black footed ferret, heath hen, passenger pigeon, and woolly mammoth.

In other research developments, scientists are now growing Neanderthal/human hybrid brains in a lab. Professor Svante Paabo, an evolutionary geneticist at the Max Planck Institute for Evolutionary Anthropology and author of *Neanderthal Man: In Search of Lost Genomes,* has already led an international team of scientists to successfully unravel the Neanderthal genome. To this end, the team has been using CRISPER gene-editing techniques to study the development of brains to determine what makes us human.

This goal of bringing back the Neanderthals is even closer to reality through the Neanderthal Genome Project, a collaboration involving several U.S. companies, scientists, and Germany's Max Planck Institute. As described in a *Science* article, "Can We Bring Neanderthals Back" by Robert Lamb, the process involves extracting DNA from bones, removing any contaminant DNA from bacteria or humans, and reconstructing the genome from decayed and chemically altered fragments. The artificial DNA then needs to be packaged into a cell, a process being developed. Alternatively, if DNA is put into a stem cell, it can be cultured and implanted into a human or blastocyst, a structure that exists very early when the embryo first develops.

Then, the resulting embryo is a mix of mostly Neanderthal and some human features.

Thus, bringing back the Neanderthal is scientifically possible. George Church, the Harvard geneticist, believes cloning a Neanderthal in our lifetime might occur, using current stem cell technology and a completed sequence of the Neanderthal genome. The procedure involves inserting a cell with the DNA from Neanderthal bones and nurturing it in the body of a human female or in a lab environment. Then, nine months later, a Neanderthal baby!

Though scientists have not yet produced a Neanderthal baby, the research shows it is possible. For instance, scientists have been studying the effects of Neanderthal genes in human tissues, and they have already created mice with Neanderthal genes. Soon they will have Neanderthal cell lines, tissues, and organs.

What Happens If We Bring Back the Neanderthals?

Since a Neanderthal baby is in the realm of possibility, scientists have started debating the ethics of doing so. One example is the controversy swirling around a scientist in China, He Jiankui, who edited the human genome to produce twin girls. Once his work became known, this provoked a scandal, because he flouted the current norms for safety and human protections. One major concern was that he could have inadvertently caused mutations in other parts of the genome, causing unpredictable health consequences, though Jiankui claimed he found no such mutations. Given this disapproval by the scientific community, Jiankui was censured by the Guandong health ministry where he worked, and he was fired from his university for inadequate safety testing and not following standard procedures.

Jiankui's story shows that the idea of producing a Neanderthal baby is highly controversial. Yet it is still likely to happen, like most new breakthroughs in science, because a few courageous scientists are likely to work with the new technologies before they are accepted. In fact, if their scientific efforts are successful, their breakthrough will likely lead to further debate and eventual acceptance.

Once any Neanderthals do return, some of the questions raised are the following:

- Will they be able to eat a regular human diet, since they might not have the necessary mutations to digest dairy products and processed grains?
- Will they be susceptible to common diseases or pathogens to which humans are immune?
- Will they enjoy a decent quality of life?
- If the Neanderthal is naturally aggressive? How can that be controlled?
- What kind of habitat will be most suitable for Neanderthals, since humans have taken over the once prime habitats where they used to live?
- Since humans played a major role in the original extinction of Neanderthals by competing with them for food and homes and maybe giving them lethal diseases, will we cause them to become extinct again?
- What will happen if humans and Neanderthals interbreed to create half-human, half-Neanderthal babies?
- Once Neanderthals are raised outside of scientific labs and facilities, where will they live? Will they live in group homes? With adoptive families?
- Will Neanderthals be able to live independently when they grow up?
- Will Neanderthals be given the rights of ordinary humans or be treated more like animals or pets?
- How should a Neanderthal child be cared for?

- How will Neanderthals be educated to adapt to a modern society? Should a Neanderthal child be put in a nursery school and later in elementary school?
- How will modern humans react to Neanderthals in the community?
- What kind of jobs can Neanderthals do, assuming their lower intelligence and aggressive nature?
- What will happen if a Neanderthal commits a crime, though they may not understand our ideas about crimes?
- What will happen if a Neanderthal becomes a victim of a crime?
- Will Neanderthals become a new underclass of society, who may easily become poor underpaid workers or even slaves?

Introducing the Neanderthal Stories

In sum, there are many issues that will occur if Neanderthals are brought back to modern society. I have written this book of fictional stories after thinking about these different issues. The stories are based on the premise that scientists can bring back the Neanderthals, initially raise them in special facilities, and thereafter find them a place to live in a local community, where they face some of these issues and more.

More specifically, *The Return of the Neanderthals* is a series of interconnected stories based on the initial premise that a paleontologist brings back some DNA from a Neanderthal burial ground discovered in an archeological dig in Northern Europe. He then works with a scientist friend to bring back six Neanderthal babies using stem cell, cloning, and CRISPER techniques, along with the help of some surrogate mothers.

These Neanderthal babies are raised in secret for their first few years of life in a laboratory setting, with the help of a nursery school teacher who teaches them basic skills. They learn some simple language skills and tasks, and when they are five or six, the scientists place them in a group home for kids with disabilities. Meanwhile, a sociologist learns about their research and raises concerns about how the Neanderthals are being treated. Later, while they are in the group home, their secret is revealed after an unexpected incident brings in the cops and the media.

As the Neanderthals grow up from childhood through young adulthood, these stories look at what happens to the Neanderthals and those who live with them, care for them, employ them, or interact with them in school, at work, and in public events as they experience the challenges of everyday life.

Along the way, they go to school, have relationships as teenagers, fall in love with other Neanderthals and sometimes humans, and start working in unskilled jobs. Some even benefit from getting a genius pill which makes them smart for a while. Like any small distinct population, they face problems of bullying, prejudice, exploitation, and discrimination, though many fight back, and some modern humans take up their cause.

The New Neanderthals Police Force continues this story as other scientists and CEOs in other parts of the country and around the world bring back Neanderthals. They do so by variously creating or obtaining embryos, buying Neanderthal babies or infants, or in some cases trafficking in Neanderthals.

They bring back the Neanderthals for various purposes -- such as to do hard, routine work in factories and fields rather than using robots, Others might use the Neanderthals for entertainment or sports, such as featuring them in boxing and wrestling matches or playing football or in a new Neanderthal football league. And some government officials might take advantage of the Neanderthals' strength, power, and good vision to use them in police and military activities.

One man who decides to use the Neanderthals as workers is the owner of a robot factory, who learns about the success of the first group of Neanderthals. He decides to create a workforce of Neanderthals to replace the robots in his factory and shipping facility. After that program proves successful and word of it spreads, some detectives think the Neanderthals could help them in crime fighting, because of their strength, aggressiveness, and hunting skills. So they recruit and train a team of six Neanderthals to help them find and capture elusive criminals, when the usual law enforcement methods fail. In their first assignment, they track down an escaped convict who has fled into the desert and the mountains beyond it. Once the Neanderthals prove their worth, the team tackles other assignments for the cops, and they face challenges and danger along the way.

The New Neanderthals Gang builds on this story, when a criminal gang leader learns about the Neanderthals working for the cops, and he decides to create his own gang of Neanderthals to commit crimes for profit and revenge and to thwart the efforts of the Neanderthals helping the cops. He obtains the Neanderthal children from individuals and organizations that are raising and taking care of them around the country. As these Neanderthal children grow up, they learn the skills to become criminals in a gang, just as the members New Neanderthals Police Force learned how to become crime fighters.

The chapters in this book introduce three different groups of Neanderthals who have become part of the modern world. Now, I invite you to meet the Neanderthals and experience their stories.

PART I: THE NEANDERTHALS ARE BACK: THE BEGINNING

CHAPTER 1: DISCOVERY

It was another snowy day in northern Germany. Darryl Jonas pulled the canvas doors of his tent back, hoping the storm would break soon, so the team of paleontologists he headed could return to the field and continue digging. They had already found some fossilized logs and ash, suggesting an ancient campfire of the Neanderthals. He was hopeful the crew could find some burial artefacts, even some remains of bones, once they could start digging again.

Darryl lit his lamp with a match and sat back on his sleeping bag. As he often did in these quiet alone moments, he pulled out his small binder with photos of his wife Annie and two kids, 4-year old Sammy and 6 year-old Jimmy. Just gazing at them made him feel better, like a reminder of why he continued to do this difficult work, because he had the support of his family, as well as his dedication to science and desire to do something more to stand out and be honored in his field.

"Yes, I know you're all still here for me," he thought as he moved the photo up and down between his hands, like the movement was making the image seem even more present and alive.

He thought about their last day, before he flew to Germany. They had gone to the county fair for an exciting fun-filled day, so they would have that lasting memory of him while he was gone for six weeks. Also, he wanted to enjoy an exhilarating last day with his wife, so there would be no time for regrets and talks about how much they would each miss each other while he was gone. Now more than ever, he felt that yearning for her, as he pulled his parka closer around him to keep out the cold.

He blew out the light and settled back in his sleeping back, hopeful that tonight would be the last of the storm, and they could continue to chip away at the remains of an ancient campfire they had discovered earlier that day. What else might it contain of the Neanderthal past?

He fell asleep dreaming of the campfire, and in the flames he saw the faces of his wife and kids smiling their encouragement for him to keep on digging. "We dig what you are doing," their faces seemed to say, as they danced in the flames.

* * * * * * *

In the morning, as Darryl peered out of his tent, the snow sparkled in the sun and he was relieved the storm was over. He met his three teammates - Fred, Duke, and Jim -- by a roaring fire where they had started to cook up a breakfast of eggs and coffee. Then, they headed to the cave with the logs and ash. With their shovels, they quickly pushed away the banks of snow in front of the path, and next used their small picks and tweezers to carefully dig through the mounds of ash and dirt around the remains of the ancient campfire.

They dug quietly, carefully, as if they were meditating in a state of reverence for the ancient treasures they might find. It was also a way to imagine what life might have been way back then in order to better consider what they might find.

Suddenly, Darryl's pick struck something hard.

"I think I have something," he yelled out.

All eyes turned to him, and the others watched in silence, as he continue to pick carefully at the dirt, pushing it away into a small pile they would later remove from the cave.

Finally, Darryl saw it, a fragment of bone. As he dug a little more, he saw a dozen other bones. He imagined they were probably placed together in a common burial site, perhaps with some kind of ritual recognizing their death and maybe even praying for their soul to travel to another world for another life somewhere. Or was he just hoping for that outcome, imagining that the Neanderthals might have had the beginnings of faith

16

that drew them together as they buried other Neanderthals in what he now believed must have been a group grave.

Eagerly he kept digging with his pick and tweezer, as his teammates spoke enthusiastically, encouraging him to keep going.

"Way to go!"

"Dig on!"

Once the pit with the bones was exposed, he pulled them out, placing each one, like an honored trophy, in a bag to take back to the lab for further analysis.

"It's a real breakthrough," Fred commented.

"It shows we are on the right track," said Duke.

"Yes," Darryl agreed. "It's like a reward for our months of hard work digging here."

"And it shows we were right," Jim observed. "That's because we choose the location we did based on the rocks and caves suggesting this might be an ideal spot to find Neanderthal remains."

Later that day, after a lunch of dried apricots and beef jerky, they continued digging and bagged more bones and chipped rocks, suggesting the Neanderthals might have created simple tools. Once it grew dark, they toasted their success around a fire by their tents. Though they weren't in a cave, their night of celebration echoed the success the Neanderthals might have had after they brought back game in a hunt.

"Just think what our professors will say," Fred said.

"And the media," said Jim.

"Yes, it'll be great to get some well-deserved glory," Duke agreed. He turned to Darryl. "And you deserve it most of the credit as our team leader and the one who first found the bones."

"But anyone of us could have found them," said Darryl. "We were all digging in the same area together. Anyone of us could have first uncovered the bones."

For a few hours, they went on toasting and celebrating each other for their find. It was just a few small bones, but they shone a light on the life of the Neanderthals many thousands and thousands of years ago.

* * * * * *

Back home, after a day of picnicking, walking around a nearby lake, and playing ball in the backyard with Annie and the kids, Darryl headed over to the lab at the university. He carried the bag with the bones, each one preserved in its own inner bag, and he met with Jeremy, the lab director.

"We'd like you to do some age tests, to determine how old these bones are," Darryl said. "Then, we'd like you to arrange for some DNA testing in order to establish that these are, in fact, Neanderthal bones."

"Certainly," Jeremy agreed. "We can sequence each genome and do some comparisons with human DNA to see the segments where the Neanderthal DNA differs."

"Sound good," Darryl agreed.

As he was about to leave, Jeremy stopped him.

"Look, you've been so successful in collecting these bones, I'd like to suggest an experiment we could do with them."

Darryl turned back. "What kind of experiment."

"Well, it could be a real breakthrough, though we'll have to keep it secret at first."

Darryl was intrigued, yet hesitant and suspicious.

"What do you mean a secret breakthrough?"

"This. It's something I've been thinking about since I've read about the new developments with gene editing through the CRISPR gene editing tools and the new procedures of inserting cells from monkeys into mice to make the mice smarter. Other researchers have been using stem cell therapy to cure diseases and prolong life. Some scientists have been successful in cloning several different types of mammals, including dogs and cats. And

18

recently scientists have brought back all sorts of once extinct mammals, such as the Tasmanian tiger, and now there are plans to de-extinct a mammoth."

"Now I'm intrigued. What are you thinking?"

"Here's my idea. You've got all of these bones from Neanderthals. I just need a single bone. I can extract the DNA, insert it into a human stem cell, and then with a human surrogate, we end up with a Neanderthal child with just a very tiny percentage of human DNA left over from the stem cell. What do you think?"

Darryl lapsed into silence. He wasn't sure what to think.

"I don't know. Is it legal to do this? Is it ethical?" he asked finally.

"Look, just about any scientific breakthrough pushes past what's currently known and legal at the time. That's because the breakthrough is so new and innovative. But after it's successful, it gains acceptance and the laws change to accommodate it."

Again, Darryl was silent, thinking.

Jeremy continued. "Just think of all the things we wouldn't have, if scientists and inventors hadn't pushed the barriers of what was then commonly known and accepted. Penicillin. Human flight. You name it. Humans even expanded from Africa to live all over the globe."

Finally, Darryl nodded.

"So if we do this, what are you proposing?"

"I just need one bone to extract some DNA. Then, I'll use some stem cells and insert the DNA into the cells to clone it. I'll take care of finding a woman who will be our surrogate. Then, we can raise the child in one of our facilities. And if that works, we can use more DNA from that bone or other bones, so we can create both male and female Neanderthal babies."

"What happens as they grow up?"

"Don't worry. We'll deal with all that when it happens. For now we'll just see if this new technology works. So what do you say?"

Uncertainly, Darryl glanced at the bones he was holding. He thought back to the hard days of digging in Norway. He saw himself playing with Annie and the kids in the backyard. And he imagined the cheering of crowds to celebrate a scientific breakthrough he might create, so he and Jeremy might be like Newton, Galileo, Edison, and other famous scientists who changed the world.

"Okay," he said finally. "I'll do it. So let's begin. I'm still not totally sure about doing this. But I'm willing to take a chance and see what happens."

He handed the bag of bones to Jeremy. Jeremy took it and squeezed Darryl's hand.

"Good. I'll get started and I'm sure everything will be fine."

But would it? Darryl left, still uncertain, yet intrigued, curious to see how things would turn out.

CHAPTER 2: THE FIRST YEARS

Afraid that the secret of the experiment would get out and the project would be shut down before it even started, Darryl decided not to contact any of their associates for referrals to a surrogate mother. They knew how unkind established scientists could be to science that broke through traditional practices and procedures. And the media, that loves a controversy and scandal, would play up the dispute and their hope of doing a study that combined care for any Neanderthal children that were born with the same kind of loving care and compassion provided to any child, even if very different.

So they got a box at a post office box in a nearby town and put an ad in Craigslist for surrogate mothers.

"Let's see if we can get six of them," Jeremy suggested, "and get a few extra surrogates in case any of the first group back out"

"And let's try to get boys and girls," Darryl said. "That way we can compare their development and how they learn, and compare that with other research on the differences in males and females in their early years."

"Agreed," Jeremy said, "and we should be able to tell in the very earliest days of the pregnancy about the sex of the fetus, so we can control for that."

And so Darryl set about placing the ad, requesting women from 18 to 30 who were interested in participating in a scientific experiment as surrogate mothers. "And you have to be willing to keep your surrogacy a secret and be willing to live in a comfortable country setting."

So what kind of response would they get? At first, Darryl and Jerome were worried no one would apply or the women wouldn't be appropriate.

"What if the requirement for secrecy or living in an isolated setting would keep anyone from applying. But a few days later, they knew they didn't have to worry, since they got several dozen responses from women who included their photos and write sincere heartfelt letters about why they wanted to apply.

Several women said they liked the seclusion since they hoped to get away from abusive husbands or boyfriends. A few women said they had been struggling to get jobs. Two women had previously been surrogate mothers, and they loved the experience of being pregnant and the feeling they were helping women who couldn't get pregnant, though they felt sad when they had to give up the child. One woman who had just graduated from college wasn't sure what she wanted to do next, and this would help her take some time off before she had to get a regular job and decide on what she wanted to do as a career.

When the women arrived for their interviews in an office the rented in an office building near their post office box, Darryl and Jeremy first gave them non-disclosure firms.

"You understand you can't talk about this project with anyone, including this interview. Do you understand?" asked Darryl.

The women readily agreed, and then Darryl and Jeremy spoke in general terms about the project, explaining that it was for a study on child development for a special population of children.

"And you'll have to agree to give up the child immediately after its birth," Darryl said. "You won't even be able to see or hold the child."

"But you'll be very well cared for by a team of nurses and midwives. It'll be like you're staying in a country club, with your own private room and various amenities, such as a nice backyards and nearby woods you can explore and a woods you can swim in.

Then, if Darryl and Jeremy thought the woman was good fit with an easy going personality and was agreeable, they brought in one of the nurses or midwives they had recruited by similarly placing an aid on Craigslist to join a team of women caring for six surrogate women for about 20-30 hours a week at a country home. Fortunately, Darryl had inherited such a home, so that would be the perfect setting. And then after the babies were born, the plan was for the nurses and midwives to care for the children in their first few years, and give reports every few days to Darryl and Jeremy about how the children were doing.

* * * * * *

After two months, the interviews were concluded and the experiment began. As they had been instructed, the three nurses and midwives hired to care for the children regularly picked them up, hugged them, and showed how much they cared for them, though the switched who cared for which child, so they wouldn't get overly attached, and the children would learn to take multiple caretakers for granted. They had regular meetings with Darryl and Jeremy to tell them how well things were going, and this gave Darryl and Jeremy a chance to meet with and hold and hug the children, too.

"I feel like their father," Jeremy commented at the first session.

"And you are. It's like we both are," Darryl observed. "It's like all of us are their foster parents. And then as they get older they will get other parents at a group home."

* * * * * * * *

After a few months, the children were ready to start crawling, and the nurses and midwives, Betsy, Sharon, and Janice, had some observations to share with Darryl and Jeremy.

"I've been noticing how the kids seem to be developing different personalities," said Betsy. "One of the boys, we call Joe, always seems to be faster than the other kids. Like he's in a race

23

to show he can get across the room or from one place to another first."

"And one of the girls, we call Marcy, is like that, too," said Sharon. "Like she's a real show off and wants to show everyone how skilled she is."

"Also, one of the boys, we call Davy, and one of the girls, we call Kim, seem to be the social butterflies of the group. They are frequently going around hugging others and smiling at them," Janice added. "And then the other two children, Bobby and Suzie, seem shy, like they are more often crawling around alone."

"That's interesting," Darryl observed. "We'll have to see if those different personality patterns continue as they get old, and I feel certain they will. After all, in modern human children mothers, nurses, and others notice such differences early on. It's like some children are born leaders and others develop their personality traits quite early."

CHAPTER 3: LEARNING IN THE LAB

After a few years, Darryl and his scientist friend Jeremy had a half-dozen Neanderthal children who were three or four years old playing in a small house in Jim's backyard.   Three were boys and three were girls, since Darryl and Jeremey felt that would be the best way to compare them as they grew up.

Jeremy brought in some toys they could play with -- a mix of dog throw, squeeze, and chew toys, and some small children's toys -- Lego blocks, soft fluffy Nerf balls, cotton-filled Raggedy Ann and Andy dolls, and some Styrofoam hoops, Frisbees, and swords.

"Now let's see what they do with them," Jeremy said.

For several months they simply observed from the side of the room or through the mirror from an adjacent room. They took careful notes to report each child's progress.

Then, at weekly meetings, they discussed the children's progress.

"They seem to be especially aggressive," noted Darryl at one of these meetings.

"That's right," said Jeremy. "And that goes for the girls as well as the boys. They don't pick up and nurture dolls like other little girls do at a young age. They just throw them around like the boys do. And they play wrestle with them, too."

"Yeah, they're tough little things," Darryl agreed. "So maybe we need to have someone teach them how to be more nurturing."

"Right. They all need someone to help teach and guide them on some basic skills to learn as they grow up."

So Darryl and Jim brought in a nursery school teacher by interviewing several candidates and pledged them to secrecy.

They first brought in Marcy Wilshire, but after she listed her sterling credentials of working at several schools around the country, she spoke about letting children freely explore and observe on their own.

"Every child needs to play and discover whatever they want to discover. You don't have to formally teach them. Instead, their natural curiosity leads them to learn what's important, and they model their behavior after you."

As Marcy droned on, Darryl and Jeremy looked at each other, both knowing she wouldn't work out. Her approach offered no direction or guidance, which seemed too chaotic to them. When she finished her lecture on the need to let children find themselves on their own, Jeremy politely told her: "Thank you, Ms. Wilshire. We'll get back to you."

They never did.

Then, there was Janice Cotton, and they immediately knew she wouldn't work out either, because she was too strict about discipline. After Darryl asked her: "What do you think is the most important thing to instill in a young child?" she responded:

"You've got to show them who's boss from an early age. So I want to make sure the children quickly follow my orders about when to wash, when to go to bed, when to get up, when to do a few small assigned chores. They need to know from the outset what you expect, and if they don't follow your instructions, they need to know there will be consequences."

"What consequences?" asked Jeremy, already knowing he wouldn't let Janice within a few feet of the children.

"Well, they won't get their usual treats the first time they misbehave. Then, they might not get dessert with their next meal. Oh, and I'd tell them why they are being punished each time. After that, they might have to stand in a corner during their playtime. Perhaps they might be spanked a little, too, although I have found that standing in a corner is usually the last thing I need to do. After that they know to behave or else."

"Thank you very much, Ms. Cotton," Darryl said at the end of her diatribe. Then she was gone.

But everything was different when Sarah Loomly arrived, and Darryl and Jeremy knew she was the one, after she answered their question about what she thought was most important for working with young children who don't have parents to raise them.

"You have to show them love," she said. "You have to show them care and compassion. You have to show them you really value them, and you have to guide them in how to behave. For example, you give them examples of what to do."

"What if they don't do what you want?" Jeremy asked.

"Then, you show them how to do it again, and when they do it right you give them an award. You reward them rather than punish them, and if they do something wrong, you distract them so they do something else. Then you show them what you want them to do right again. This shows the children what is a good thing to do and what is not. So it gently leads them to learn."

"Very good," said Jeremy. "I like those answers."

Then Darryl and Jeremy had to make sure Sarah understood the importance of keeping everything confidential.

"You will be teaching some very special children," Jeremy explained. "They look different and act different, and they may be slow to learn and maybe more aggressive than most children. Do you think you can handle that?"

"Oh, yes," Sarah assured them. "I've trained children from all kinds of families -- from wealthy families and from some from middle income and poor families, who wanted the best for their children. And a few children were on the autism spectrum, so I had to pay special attention to their different way of perceiving and understanding things and their unique way of expressing themselves."

Finally, it was time to tell Sarah the secret of the program and introduce her to the children.

Darryl pulled a non-disclosure form out of a briefcase.

"We have an NDA for you to fill out," he explained. "You have to keep secret what we are doing here. You can't tell anyone, even your closest friends, husband, or family members."

"Of course," Sarah agreed and quickly signed the form.

"There, I signed it," she said.

After that, Jeremy explained about the children. "They're Neanderthals. They were brought back through the process of cloning ancient cells. Now we want to give them the best life possible today, and we need your help. We want you to train and educate them as best you can. It's the first time anyone has done this, and we can't let anyone know."

"I understand," Sarah said. "And I'll honor your request. I'm honored to be part of an experiment of this magnitude. So no worries."

"Good," said Jeremy.

Then, he led her into the room in the lab where the six children were playing, mostly squeezing their toys, throwing them around, chasing after them, and engaging in play wrestling matches.

Sarah gazed at the playing children for a few minutes, then observed, "Well, I can see I have my work cut out for me. When shall I begin."

"Now," said Jeremy. "And if you need any help from us, just ask. We're ready to help you all we can."

"Good," said Sarah and she went over to greet the children. They looked up, and she said simply, "I'm Sarah," pointing to herself to reinforce her message. Then, gesturing around the room and to herself, she said, "I'll be your teacher."

She hoped by sharing her message in signs as well as words that the children would come to understand what she was saying and maybe learn to speak themselves. She knew it would be difficult, but she thought of how Penny Patterson had taught Koko the gorilla to learn sign language. Maybe she could learn something from that.

She then watched as the children went back to playing, like she wasn't there. She felt that would be the first step -- getting accustomed to her being there. After that, she could start using treats and rewards to help them learn how to understand and speak different things. It would be a process of discovery, and she was ready to guide them along the way.

Darryl and Jeremy watched her from the corner of a room, feeling confident that they had made the right choice of the Neanderthals' teacher.

CHAPTER 4: LEAVING THE LAB

After Sarah had been working with the Neanderthal kids for a year, Darryl and Jeremy felt it was time to move them to a home environment.

"They have to learn to become part of the community," Jeremy said.

"Agreed," said Darryl.

So what did the kids know? How could they function outside of the lab?

Darryl and Jeremy asked Sarah to join them in the office near the playroom where she worked with the kids.

"What's up," she asked.

"We want to find out how well they are doing. We'd like to have the kids raised in a home in the community, and we'd like to see if they are ready," Jeremy said.

"What do you think?" Darryl asked.

"They definitely behave much better," Sarah said. "They have mostly stopped fighting with each other, except maybe over a particular toy that both want. But I have learned how to stop them by separating the fight. Then, I either give them a second toy, or I'll tell one of the fighters he can play with the toy for a few minutes, and then he has to give the toy to the other person to play with. They seem to understand what I am saying and agree."

"That's encouraging," said Jeremy.

"Yes. And they have learned certain words and ideas, such as if I ask a boy or girl to get me a certain flower of a certain color. Or I might ask a child to move something from one place to another, or I can create a race where the kids will try to be the first to do something, like build a small house with logs."

"So they understand some words and simple commands," Darryl observed.

"Yes. That's right," Sarah said. "And I have taught them how to eat with utensils, so they use forks, spoons, and knives, instead of grabbing everything with their hands or slurping things from bowls."

Sarah glanced around the room and pointed to some simple pictures with color splotches on the walls.

"And they can create small works of art, too. They have a sense of pattern and design."

Sarah pointed to three children gathered around a plant. "They have learned to take care of plants, too. I give them water and they water it every day."

Sarah continued on with other examples.

At the end, Darryl stated: "It sounds like you think they're ready."

"Yes, I do. Though I have a concern about their speaking ability. I did some research on Neanderthals, and the position of their tongue and mouth is a bit different from humans today. Their larynx may be a little different, too. So that might make it more difficult for them to speak as we do, though scientists aren't sure about this. "

Darryl looked thoughtful. "Well, maybe or maybe not. But I'm sure we can fix that with modern technology. After all, there are devices now that enable humans to turn their thoughts into words or use their thoughts to send directions to a computer. So why not this?"

"Well, maybe that might work. But another problem is that they might tend to be more aggressive and impulsive, because of what some scientists call the "brawn over brain" theory. So maybe they might be more likely to get into fights than other children."

Again Darryl looked thoughtful, as he considered the possibilities.

"I think we can resolve that problem, too. After all, people in some cultures tend to be more emotional and expressive, such as in Italy and Mexico, while others tend to have a more reserved and rational approach to life, such as in Germany and Scandanavia. And individuals within a culture also differ in whether they are more likely to respond aggressively when they feel anger or can hold back and control those feelings. So these different ways of responding can be learned."

"I guess that's true," Sarah replied. "So on that basis, I think it would be good for them to go to a home. It'll get them out of this isolation in a single room where they only see and interact with each other and me. And it can show them how to behave with other children and adults."

So it was decided. The Neanderthal children would soon leave the sanctity of the lab. But where would they go?

Darryl began making calls to local home care facilities and group homes, asking if they could take on six special needs kids. "What kind of special needs?" was the usual question the facility owners or managers asked. Darryl didn't want to say exactly what these kids were like, not yet, until he had picked out a good place and swore the owner or manager to secrecy with an NDA. So he simply compared the children to kids who were slightly retarded with Down Syndrome or Asperger's Syndrome, since he wasn't sure what other category they might fit into.

A few centers said no, they had all the kids they could successfully handle right now. Some others had run into financial difficulties, since their funders lost interest in their facilities and had invested in something else, so now they were closing and couldn't take on more kids.

But finally they reached Dan Newfounder, who had a facility in the countryside just beyond a small suburban city. He specialized in taking in special needs kids who had been abandoned by their parents because of their difficult to handle disabilities.

"What do you do for them? How do you teach them?" Darryl asked.

"We help them adjust to society," Dan explained. "So we teach them how to socialize with others. And we prepare them to work in simple jobs, such as in rehab workshops, on farms, in factories, and on ranches. Then, we can see how the kids respond, and decide changes might be advisable."

"Sounds like a good approach," Dan said.

A few days later, Darryl and Jeremy went out to visit the facility with Sarah to make sure this would be right place for the kids.

"How old are the kids?" Sarah asked, as they walked around the grounds and saw several kids feeding the cows in the barn.

"Anywhere from 2 to 8," Dan said. "Though most are 5 or 6 now. Later, after we determine their capabilities, we can look for a center for older kids. Or sometimes we search for families who would like to adopt and care for special needs kids."

When they returned to Dan's office, Jeremy handed Dan the NDA form. After Dan signed, Jeremy explained about the Neanderthal project.

"Of course, it's a big secret," he concluded. "No one can know. Just treat them like regular kids with special needs and tell others the same thing. When the time is right, we'll tell the world, but that's not now. Let's see how far they can developed when they're exposed to more human contact in a safe, supportive environment, before they might be exposed to discrimination by other humans. "

"Understood," said Dan. "Your secret's safe with me. I only want to do what's best for the kids."

"Good," said Darryl. "We need to avoid any special attention. We don't want the kids to grow up in a fish bowl of media attention and government bureaucracy. That's what would happen if the word gets out now."

"Of course," said Dan. "You have my word. No one will know. Not even the neighbors. And we're pretty isolated out here in the country, which should be ideal."

So it was done. After they got back to the lab, Darryl and Jeremy started making preparations to transfer the kids, and Sarah agreed to help get them ready for the big move.

Then, the day before the move, Darryl's assistant Tanya called the lab to say, "There's a sociologist Jackie Wills here to see you."

"I'm too busy," Darryl replied on the intercom. "Just get her number and say I'll call her back in a few days after we move."

"But Ms. Wills says it's very urgent. She wants to talk to you about the Neanderthal project."

"What?" Darryl replied, suddenly very anxious. "No one is supposed to know about this. How the hell could she...?"

For a few moments, Tanya was silent, as she spoke to Jackie. Finally, she came back on the line.

"Jackie says she'll tell you when she speaks to you,"

Darryl put the phone on mute and turned to Jeremy. "This woman knows about the project."

"Oh, my God, no!!" Jeremy said. "It's too soon. We can't let this get out. It might destroy everything."

Darryl nodded. "Okay. We better talk to her."

He turned back to the phone and unmuted it. "Okay, send her up, Tanya,"

A few minutes later, Jackie was sitting across from Darryl and Jeremy, a briefcase in her lap.

"I'm here because I'm concerned about your project," Jackie began.

"How do you know about it?"

"That's not important."

"But it is. It's supposed to be secret, until the time is right to reveal it.

"Oh, And you're afraid of the secret getting out now, because it might be stopped."

"Yes, and we still have so much to learn."

"But have you considered the project's impact on human lives? You're treating the kids like rats in a cage and seeing how they respond to different stimuli."

"No, that's not true," Jeremy said. "We want to protect and support the kids. That's why we need to keep this secret until they are old enough...."

"For what?" Jackie said. "So you can exploit them? Treat them like pets in a zoo for people to see? Create films about them to make money..."

"No. None of that," Darryl said. "We just want to see if Neanderthals can grow up in modern society like other humans, when they're given an education and introduced to other children and adults."

"And what if they don't adjust as you hoped?"

"Then they can be treated like the differently-abled," Jeremy said.

"Oh, you think it's going to be that easy. What happens if they are discriminated against, mocked, made fun of? How do you expect to handle that? Have you considered that this whole experiment might be considered unethical? It's like you are bringing up a whole generation who are like slaves in captivity, And they don't have any parents to love and care for them, so you're holding onto them like jailers."

"My God! How can you think that?" Darryl said. "We want to find loving care for them, even adoptive parents, when they're ready. Anyway, just who are you to lecture us on what to do, and how do you know about what we are doing? Everyone involved has been pledged to the strictest confidence and signed NDAs. So who?"

"No one told me, if that's what concerns you. I just happened to be in a café, when you were making arrangements about taking the kids to a group home. Then, the woman you were talking to left her phone on the table, when she went to pick up her lunch, and I saw how you texted her your address. So that's how I know."

"Then, who...? Darryl began.

Jackie continued. "As for who I am, I'm a sociologist at the university in town, and I teach about social justice and social change. So I'm very concerned about ethics. Plus I'm involved in the movement to protect immigrant rights, and I can see how a new generation of Neanderthals could be treated like immigrants or some disadvantaged minority group. So their human rights could be an issue, too. And there are ethical considerations when anyone is a test subject."

Darryl and Jeremy looked at each other uncertainly, unsure what to do.

"Then, what do you want? To expose the project? To stop it?" Darryl asked. "Look, the kids are already here, and it'll be worse for them, if they are suddenly in the public eye."

"Yeah, they'd be treated like circus animals, and that would be the end of any opportunities to learn and grow in human society," Jeremy added.

"Okay then. I won't say anything to anyone -- for now. But I need your pledge in return that kids will be raised like they are ordinary kids, who need love and nurturing from any adults who are taking care of them."

"We can certainly do that," said Jeremy.

"And you need to make sure that anyone you entrust with their care does this, too."

"Yes, we agree," Jeremy said.

"And you won't try to exploit them or show them off like exhibits in a fair, film, or product ad."

"Yes, we agree to that, too," Darry said.

"And you have to keep me informed, so I know where the kids are and I can see them from time to time."

Darryl and Jeremy hesitated, then nodded,

"Yes, we agree," Jeremy said.

"Okay, then," said Jackie. "We're agreed."

Jackie stood up. "So now I'll be watching to check on how things are going. And if I see that you haven't followed our agreement or aredoing anything unethical, I'll be back on your case, and I'll...

Jackie left the thought unspoken as she turned to leave. Darryl called out to her and she stopped.

"You'll do what?"

Jackie hesitated thoughtfully, then replied. "Well, we'll just have to see."

Finally, she turned and walked out.

Darryl and Jeremy turned to each other nervously.

"Jesus, we've got a watchdog on our case," Darryl said.

"I know. That's all we need now. God, let's hope that nothing goes wrong."

* * * * * * * *

The following day, Jeremy led the kids from the lab on a small chartered bus. Darryl sat behind the driver, a burly man who looked like a retired boxer, and he greeted each boy or girl as they got onto the bus.

"Hi...Welcome...We're going to your new home."

Darryl wasn't sure how much the kids understood, but he felt it was important to introduce them to the world of language as soon as possible. Certainly, whatever they learned wouldn't be remotely like what the Neanderthals did in the forests or tundra of Norway so many thousands of years ago. But at least this would be a way to find out how much they could learn and how well they could adjust in their new world.

Meanwhile, as the kids mounted the stairs to the bus and found seats along the sides, they looked around nervously, as if scanning for predators in this strange environment. Then, with Jeremy guiding them, they sat down, one on either side of each row. As the bus started up, they whispered among themselves and looked around some more, even looking up at the top of the bus, as if they expected an animal might be hiding there ready to jump.

"It's okay…Don't be scared…Nothing's going to hurt you," Jeremy sought to reassure them. He wasn't sure if they understood his words, but at least his soothing tone seemed to calm them. Soon they stopped searching around with their eyes and looked forward as the driver stepped on the gas and drove along the driveway leading from the building parking lot into the street.

"We're on our way now….You'll be home soon…We'll be driving through the city."

Jeremy still couldn't be sure if the kids heard or understood him or not, but he was glad to see they were now looking around with eager curiosity as the bus drove on. They tapped each other on the shoulder, grabbed another's arm, and pointed outside the window. The kids' excitement reminded him of his Golden Retriever puppy when he took it in the car for the first time. It hopped up and down in the back seat, as it looked out one window and then the other, seeing everything as new, like opening a gift box for Christmas.

Jeremy sighed with relief, feeling like this was one more sign their experiment was a success, and he glanced over at Darryl, who raised his right hand and curled his thumb and index finger into the "okay" sign.

So far so good, Jeremy and Darryl agreed. Now they just had to get the kids to the group home, where they would spend the next few years, if all went well. And hopefully the media wouldn't find out, so they and the kids could continue the experiment in peace.

CHAPTER 5: THE GROUP HOME

A half-hour later they were at the Happy Hills Group Home, a rambling brown and red ranch house, surrounded by a garden of azaleas and roses and a fortress of oak and eucalyptus trees. The owner and manager, Ernie Masters, met them at the door, ready to show them and the kids around.

As the six kids filed off the bus, he greeted them with a warm welcome.

"Welcome! Welcome! Welcome!" he said enthusiastically to each one, shaking their hands and passing them on to Maggie Waters, his recent grad school assistant, who led many of the workshops and programs.

"Maggie will show you to your rooms, and then we'll show you around."

Soon the kids were settled in, the three boys in one room with three cots, and the three girls in the other. They put down their satchels, which held a change of jeans and a few T-shirts, bounced on their beds a few times, and met Maggie, Ernie, Darryl, and Jeremy in the hallway.

"Now we'll show you around," said Ernie.

As they walked down the hall into the day room, several Down Syndrome boys and girls looked up and came over to greet them. The Neanderthal kids looked at each other quietly, uncertainly, like dogs greeting each other in a dog park.

Then, Ernie broke the ice, turning first to the boys and girls with Down Syndrome.

"Okay, kids. These will be your new neighbors. They're very special kids, just like you're very special. So get to know each other. You'll have plenty of time later, when you all play in the dayroom and at meal times, when you'll all eat together."

All the kids smiled, and Ernie walked on, relieved, as the Neanderthal kids, Maggie, Darryl, and Jeremy followed him. As they walked on, he pointed out the art room, where some children were painting large scenes of mountains and lakes with magic markers and crayons, while a few others were making large blobby clay sculptures on their desks. They passed a gym, with cardio platforms and weights lifting equipment and a big red bouncing ball. He pointed out the rec room with a ping pong table and a large TV screen on one wall. Then, they came to a small classroom with a dozen chairs and a blackboard.

"We want to give the kids an enriched learning environment," Ernie explained. "We know their abilities are limited, but we want to make life seem as normal as possible, so they are better able to adjust to life on the outside."

"Outside?" Darryl asked.

"Why yes," Ernie said. "When they grow up, if they learn to become independent, two or three of them can live together in their own apartment. They can learn to go to the grocery, even go shopping at the mall. The idea is to integrate them into everyday society as much as we can, starting with elementary school age. Then, as they get older, we have a group home for older teens and adults, and we try to help them live as independently as possible "

"That sounds great," Darryl said.

"So we have your trust?" Ernie said.

"You do," Jeremy said.

After that, Darryl and Jeremy left, feeling they had done their part in raising the Neanderthal children to this point. Now it was time for them to become mainly observers, as Ernie and Maggie brought the kids up with other children and taught them as much as they could.

"I feel like a father who just sent his kid to camp for the first time," Jeremy commented on the way back to the lab.

"Yeah," Darryl agreed. "And the more the experiment has been successful, the less they will need us."

Later that day, after the bus pulled in at the lab, Darryl headed home, eager to see his wife and kids, after so many days of quick breakfasts at home and long days at the lab.

"I'll have more time to be at home now," he told his wife Annie, as she put away things from dinner in the kitchen. "Our project just ended."

"What was that?" Annie asked.

"I can't tell you," Darryl said.

Annie looked at him with her eyes half-cocked.

"No, I don't suppose you can," she said, gave a quick scowl, and walked out the back door to the backyard.

He watched her go, uncertain about whether to go after her or what to say. He imagined himself a little like a spy just back from an assignment who has to try fitting into a regular routine again before the next assignment. So no, he couldn't tell her. It would be too easy for her to tell a friend or family member, pledging them to secrecy. Then, they would go tell someone else, in secrecy of course. And so on. So soon the secret would be out, and soon the media would come calling, and that would be the end of an experiment to see if the Neanderthal kids could grow up to live normal lives.

But what could he do to get back in Annie's good graces. Flowers? A nice dinner? He wasn't sure, thinking such gifts would make it seem like he was trying to come back from an ended affair with a mistress. So what?

He went to the window and looked out on Annie puttering around in the garden, while the kids threw balls and jumped on the backyard trampoline.

What could he do? For now he felt very much alone, and he thought of the Neanderthal kids. Maybe they were not part of society yet. But at least they had each other and some other kids they could get to know at the group home, as they tried to learn how to become a part of ordinary life.

At least he had been like a good dad to them for the last few years. Now it was time to move on and see how they were progressing from time to time. If only he could somehow bring Annie and his own kids back into his life the way things had been before. If only he could.

CHAPTER 6: GETTING TO KNOW THE KIDS

Over the next few days, the Neanderthal kids learned their way around the group home, and Ernie began learning their personalities. Joey was the group leader, always eager to explore new things, like the time Ernie found him running down the hall from his bedroom into the dayroom one night.

"No, you can't be here. You have to go to bed now," Ernie told him.

"Why?" asked Joey. "Not sleepy."

Ernie didn't have a really good answer and led him back to his room.

"Sleep is good for you," he explained, as he closed the door.

But early in the morning before breakfast, he found Joey back in the day room walking around and rubbing his hands over the furniture, like he was checking out a new campsite.

"Not sleepy," Joey said again.

Ernie just nodded, and Joey smiled, as if he had won the battle over turf just now.

"Wanted to see things," Joey added, and Ernie just smiled back.

"Sure. Go ahead," he said.

He dubbed Davy the people pleaser. He was always smiling and eager to be around Ernie and Maggie, as they went around doing their tasks for the day, checking on the kids in their rooms or watching them play in the dayroom and backyard. And sometimes as Davy tagged along, he would point and say:

"Me help."

Then, Ernie would find something for him to do, such as take out the lunches and place them on the table before Maggie invited everyone to come eat lunch.

Afterwards, whatever Davy did, Ernie was sure to praise him, patting him on the head and telling him:

"Very good. Good boy."

In turn, Davy raised his head up and down with even a bigger grin, and Ernie thought about how he praised his Golden Retriever Jabs with the same words and pats. Yet Davy seemed to feel real pride when he heard these words, so Ernie guessed it was okay. Kids. Dogs. Just show them you love and appreciate them, and they'll be happy and love you back.

As for Bobby, he was the shy one. He always seemed to hang back and wait to see what others in the group wanted to do. Or if Ernie asked him do something, Bobby looked around for Joey or Davy if they were nearby to see if they were going to do it, too, or agreed that he should do it. For example, one time, when Joey was banging on the piano and Davy was glancing through a picture book with dogs and cats, while Bobby sat on the couch staring off into space, Ernie went over to Bobby and asked him:

"Would you like to go outside and play ball?"

Ernie held up a big red rubber ball.

Bobby looked at the ball and then at Joey at the piano and Davy reading the book. But they didn't look back at him, and he finally nodded.

"Yes, I can play with you."

So Ernie took Bobby outside and began throwing a ball to him.

"Catch it when I throw it," Ernie said.

Ernie stepped back a few feet, and Bobby reached out his hands and tried to catch it. But at first he missed.

"That's okay," Ernie said. "I'll throw it again more slowly."

After a few more tries, Ernie urged Bobby not to be discouraged.

"Keep trying. You'll do it," he said.

After a few more throws, Bobby did catch it, and he jumped up and down excitedly, like he had just gotten a big present. He was like a little dog who had finally found a bone, and Ernie made a note to use the same techniques he did with his dog to help Bobby learn new things. Then, as he did with his Retriever, Ernie took Bobby into the kitchen and brought out a plate with a large chocolate chip cookie.

"It's for you," Ernie said. "Because you have been so good."

At once, Bobby grabbed the cookie, looked up at Ernie with a big grin and puppy dog eyes, and began tearing into the cookie like meat from a hunt.

Then, having thought about the boys, Ernie sized up the girls and noticed that they seemed very similar to the boys in many ways -- Darcy was the leader, Kim the social one, and Suzie the shy one. He also found them much like the boys in being aggressive and ready to fight back if challenged for anything, like who could play with a toy bear or who could make something with the large wooden blocks.

For example, one time he saw Darcy and Judy, one of the Down Syndrome girls, fighting about something. Judy was reaching for a Raggedy Ann doll, when Darcy grabbed it away from her.

"I want it!" Darcy said, as she pulled it away before Judy could grab it.

"No. Me play with it," Judy yelled.

Darcy pulled the doll to her chest like a baby. "No, can't have it. Mine."

Judy began to cry, and Darcy just laughed.

"Loser! Loser!" Darcy said. "So go away. Go cry someplace else. It's mine, all mine."

Darcy smiled broadly as Judy slunk away, like she had just scored a victory.

Meanwhile, Ernie continued watching, not wanting to interfere, and he wondered if Darcy would continue to cradle the doll like a little mother. But instead she grabbed the doll by the arm, twirled it around, and threw it like she was aiming a spear.

"So much for motherhood," Ernie thought, as he walked away and went outside to see what the kids were doing in the backyard.

After he came back inside, he had a chance to observe Kim, the social one, in action. She was sitting with Suzie, the shy one, and two of the Down Syndrome girls, Sheila and Patsy. She noticed the portable radio at one side of the room and brought it over, like she was presenting a deer from a kill and placed it on the small table in front of them. Then, she hit the big power button on top of the radio to turn it on. At once, the pounding beat of a rock band filled the room.

"Now let's dance," Kim said.

A moment later she was on her feet, swaying to the beat and stamping her feet. A few moments later, Sheila and Patsy joined her, while Suzie sat watching the three of them, as if she wasn't sure whether to join in or not.

For several minutes, Kim, Sheila, and Patsy moved back and forth, raising their feet a little higher, stamping them down, and jumping in the air. As Ernie noticed, Kim was always the first to start a new movement, and then the other girls followed along. But Suzie still hesitated, watching the others.

Finally, Kim came over to Suzie, bent over, and motioned for her to follow.

Willingly, Suzie did, and soon she was swaying, stamping her feet, and jumping, too, although she did so with less energy, as if she wanted to follow along to be like everyone else, yet didn't show the wild abandon of the others who seemed truly caught up in the beat of the music. Rather Suzie just mimicked them because they were doing it. But she didn't really feel free herself.

Ernie made a quick note about his observations in a small notebook, so he could remember to report what he observed to Darryl later that night. This way, though Darryl was no longer a day to day participant in the experiment, he could know what was happening. Then, he could better understand what it was like for these Neanderthal kids suddenly brought from many thousands of years ago into a new high-tech age.

CHAPTER 7: A DAY TO REMEMBER

One spring day, when the weather was warm and sunny, Ernie and Maggie took the Neanderthal kids and several Down Syndrome kids, including Judy, Sheila, and Patsy, into the backyard to draw the trees, bushes, and flowers around them. Ernie set out an easel, stool, and colored markers in front of each of them

"Now I'd like you to try drawing what you see around you. You can even draw each other."

Ernie pointed to the paintings and to the different students to make sure the children understood what he said. He picked up a few different colored markers.

"You'll use these markers to draw. Choose any color, and draw what you see."

Most of the kid quickly picked a marker and began drawing, except Suzie who sat staring ahead.

Ernie went over to her.

"What's the matter, Suzie?" Ernie asked.

"Me draw, too?" she asked.

"Yes. Of course," Ernie said. He pointed to her, then back at the board. "You draw, too."

Susie picked up a blue marker and began to draw. It was as if she just needed a personal okay to tell her to go ahead.

Ernie walked around, observing and admiring what the children were doing. Davy was painting two tree trunks, with the large eyes of an animal staring out of it. Bobby was painting a large bush with purple flowers that dotted the plant like Christmas tree lights. Darcy painted a clump of cactuses, and Ernie noticed that the spines looked especially long and dangerous, with pointed tips like spears. As a small butterfly flitted by, Darcy poked at it with her marker. It stopped stunned, and Darcy stabbed again. The butterfly tumbled down and fell on the long tray in front of her. It shook helplessly, flailing its wings, and Darcy eagerly jabbed her marker at it, finally squashing it for good. She smiled broadly, looked around and saw a few other children watching her, and nodded to them, as if acknowledging them for honoring her for her kill. Then, she turned back toward the easel and began to draw a few cactuses with dagger-like hooks.

Ernie moved, and he saw Kim and Suzie engrossed in drawing leaves, stems, and flowers.

"That's nice," he said walking over to each one. "Keep up the good work."

He patted each girl on the shoulder and walked on.

He was curious to see what Joey had drawn. Probably something tough, Ernie thought, as he passed a group of Snap Dragons, who stood like warriors, as they snapped up the flies that flew by.

After he watched a Snap Dragon munch on one of its flies, Ernie headed over to the easel at the end of the row of easels where Joey had started eagerly painting a few bushes with purple huckleberries and a shining sun between them.

But where was Joey? Ernie looked around as he stood in front of Joey's easel.

He went over to Maggie, who was watching the Judy, Kim, and Suzie sketch some flowers.

"Did you see Joey?" he asked.

"No. Why?"

"He's not at his easel."

"Maybe he got tired of panting and went inside to the dayroom or his room," Maggie replied. "Or maybe just a bathroom break."

So Ernie and Maggie went inside looking for Joey.

They looked through the dayroom and checked behind a few couches, in case Joey might be there.

They went into the gym, where a few Down Syndrome boys were lifting small weights or running on the treadmill.

"Did you see Joey?" he asked.

"No...No...No, we didn't," came a series of replies, like a chain of echoes.

Then, Ernie and Maggie headed down the corridor and looked into the room Joey shared with Davy and Bobby. But no. Not there either.

They looked in the bathroom and checked the three stalls.

"He's not in here either," Maggie said, as they headed out of the bathroom.

"Maybe he's back in the backyard drawing," Ernie suggested.

So they went back to Joey's easel and looked all around the backyard.

They stood on the patio looking stumped. Then, feeling frustrated, Ernie went up one row of easels and Maggie went up the other. They stopped besides each of the kids.

"Did you see Joey?" they asked each one, and then: "Did you see Joey go anywhere? Do you think Joey is hiding?"

Each time the kids shook their heads "no" and turned back to their easels, like they didn't want pesky grown-ups interfering with them by asking dumb questions.

But finally, Kim, whose easel was in the row behind Joey's, came over to Ernie and Maggie as they sat at the table with an umbrella on the patio.

"I saw Joey go into the bushes," Kim said. "He said it was a secret. But you looked sad, so I'm telling you."

Ernie and Maggie sat up at attention.

"I hope he won't be mad at me for telling."

"No, no, he won't be," Ernie reassured her.

"But Joey didn't come back. And I didn't want you to be sad," Kim added.

"No, we won't be now," Maggie told her.

As Kim walked back to her easel, Maggie and Ernie went out looking for Joey. They crawled through the bushes and looked around their neighbor's backyard. They drove slowly along the surrounding streets hoping they might see Joey. They stopped at a lot between two houses and walked through it. But nothing. The last thing they wanted to do was call the police and report a missing child, dreading the possibility that the media might follow once the police took the case.

They drove on some more. Then, after they stopped at the homes of a few neighbors, several neighbors drove around helping with the search.

* * * * * * *

Meanwhile, Joey emerged from the bushes into the backyard of Ernie's neighbor. He noticed a cage with two rabbits near the patio and crept up to it quietly. A dog barked from inside the house, and he grabbed a rake lying by the cage, thinking he might use it if the dog or anyone else came out of the house. But no one was home, so no one emerged from the house, and the dog soon got tired of barking and stopped.

Joey relaxed and gazed back at the rabbits hunched over in their cage.

"You don't like your cage," Joey said to the rabbits, and their ears perked up. "I don't like being in a cage either."

Joey fumbled around for a latch and opened the cage. At once the rabbits hopped out.

"Good. Go little rabbits. Free!"

The rabbits paused and gazed at Joey, their noses twitching. Then, they turned away and began running across the backyard to the bushes.

"Good. Go," Joey said again. "I go, too."

After that, he headed towards the street. Soon Joey was walking past the ranch houses that lined the block, and ahead he saw a bright red sign with six edges. He walked up to it and trailed his fingers around it and over the bright white letters that said "Stop."

After that, Joey stood by the sign watching a few cars go back and forth across the intersection.

He thought it fascinating to see the big cars in different colors -- white, black, gray, and sometimes red -- pass by, and he thought of the great big van that brought him to his home several weeks before. Then, he began counting the number of people in the cars as they passed by -- one, two, and sometimes three.

But where were the cars going so quickly? Why did some suddenly stop, while others kept going? Joey had so many questions, yet he didn't always have the words to ask them, so the fragments of thoughts kept swirling around in his head.

Better to keep on going, he thought to himself. Just see what's out there. Don't let them find you, or they'll take you back to that house with small rooms. Be free and run like the rabbits.

So Joey kept walking.

Eventually, he came to a creek bed by the side of the road and decided to follow it. It wound around like a big blue snake, with the reflections of trees crisscrossing the water as it flowed along.

As he walked along the bank, high above him, he saw the tops of the houses, like the ones he had seen on the street. But now he was down below them, and he felt like he had found a quiet little world. Around him, he noticed a few birds on a nearby bush singing. Then, a striped cat with a furry tail held high stopped across from him and stared. He stared back, as if challenging the cat to show who is boss, and the cat backed off and ran away.

A few minutes later, as he continued watching, an owl climbed out on a tree limb and gazed at him before it flapped away. And after that he saw a brown fawn emerge from the bushes on the other side of the creek. It looked at him curiously, and as he locked eyes with the fawn, it bounded away.

What a wonderful magical place, he thought. It was like a wonderful hiding place where he felt very safe, like the master of this quiet secret world.

But then, he noticed it was starting to get dark, and he felt a chill wind through his T-shirt, as the shadows of the trees began to enclose him.

Better go, he thought to himself, as he felt a twinge of fear ripple through him.

He got up and climbed up the side of hill beside the creek.

Now he was back on the street, and in the distance, he saw the sun hovering low in the sky, surrounded by a yellow-pink glow. Around him the shadows deepened. So maybe it was time to return to the safety of home, he thought. Maybe time to go back into the cage.

But where was he? And how could he get there before it became darker and darker?

Joey turned to head back the way he thought he came. But nothing looked familiar. Confused, he wondered where he was. Maybe in walking around the creek, he had gone further than he thought. Maybe he had come out on a different street. So where was he?

He heard a few cars passing back and forth at an intersection. Maybe that was the way to go. Or was it? At least at a stop sign he had seen the cars coming and going. So that's where he headed now, running faster and faster, hoping to outrun the darkening sky, so he could better find his way.

Soon Joey was at the stop sign. He looked around and saw the ranch houses with large lawns set back along the road. Each way he looked, he saw lines and lines of ranch houses, and in the growing darkness, they looked so similar. Should he turn right or left or go straight ahead to get home? He was unsure what to do, and when an occasional car whizzed by, he felt even more confused by the buzzing, whirring noises. He covered his hands over his ears, trying to shut off the noise that now throbbed in his head like a river passing through pounding rain.

Then, when he looked up, he noticed a strange projection from a tall pole. It looked a little like one of his long and silvery toy rocket ships. As he continued to watch, the strange projection flashed and beeped from time to time. So what was it? It didn't move like a bird with its wings close to its body when it wandered around looking for insects in the grass.

He stepped back to look into the eye of long, silvery projection as it occasionally flashed and beeped.

Suddenly, he heard a loud honking sound that came faster and faster. Moments later, he felt himself being pushed away and down to the street, as he crashed down hard on the concrete.   An instant later, he felt a loud rumbling explosion in his head, and when he tried to push himself up, he couldn't move. He fell back exhausted onto the concrete.

At the same time, he heard the loud roar of a car's engine, and moments later, he saw the car that struck him drive off, and he felt a crunching sound and deep stabbing pain, as the car's wheels drove over his leg.

Then,, mercifully, he felt and heard nothing more, as the world around him went dark and pulled him into a deep void.

* * * * * * *

Meanwhile, Ernie and Maggie were growing more and more frantic. As they swept through the neighborhood with a half-dozen neighbors, no Joey, nothing.

As they stood on a corner watching their neighbors, Ernie wondered: "What could have happened?"

"We've got to call the police," Maggie said.

Initially, Ernie hesitated. "I don't know. If we call the police, the media can hear about Joey gone missing on the radio. And then what? The last thing we need is to have a story about these kids out there."

"I know. But this is a kid's life we're talking about. Joey could be in danger. He could be anywhere by now, and we don't know what happened."

Finally, reluctantly, Ernie agreed "Yes, okay."

He pulled out his cell phone. Moments later he was telling the police dispatcher, "There's a missing boy. He ran off about two hours ago, and we can't find him. And now it's getting dark."

"I'll send out a patrol car," she said.

A few minutes later, a police car arrived at the scene, and Ernie and Maggie went over to him.

"We wanted to report a missing boy," Ernie began, and the officer dutifully took notes.

"We'll do what we can," he said.

Then, he called headquarters to report what he had noted, and he sent a file from his laptop to police headquarters.

Ernie and Maggie watched nervously, as the officer moved around his car with his cell phone and reached into his car to send his message. When a few neighbors who came over to find out why there was a police car on the street, they reassured them.

"He's just reporting that Joey's missing," Ernie explained. "The police will help us look."

A few minutes later, as the neighbors dispersed to their homes, since it was now night and hard to search for anything, Ernie and Maggie remained at the corner, as if transfixed, not sure what to do next.

"Maybe he'll come back on his own," Maggie suggested.

"Yeah, maybe," Ernie said. "Where could he go?"

Then, his cell phone rang, and a police officer was on the line.

Ernie's face went white as he listened.

"What's wrong?" Maggie asked.

Ernie put his phone on speaker, so she could hear the message, too.

"I'm sorry to tell you," said the police officer, "but there's been an accident. We took your report of a missing child, and then we got a report of a hit and run a few blocks away. We think it could be your boy. He's at the hospital now. Can you come and identify him?"

"Oh, my God!" Maggie shrieked, as they ran to Ernie's car.

Minutes later, they roared into the hospital parking lot, and then they were at the reception desk, telling the receptionist, "The police just called us to tell us they think our boy is here."

In moments, a nurse was in front of them saying, "Please come right this way."

After that, everything was a maze of corridors and doctors and nurses hurriedly rushing this way and that, until at last they were in the emergency unit.

"Right this way," a hospital orderly told them.

Moments later, they were in the ICU, where a doctor led them over to a boy who lay under a white sheet with tubes and wires running all over his body. But through it all they readily recognized Joey's large pumpkin-like head with heavy brow ridges.

"Yes, that's him," Ernie said, while Maggie began shaking and crying.

"How bad is it?" she sobbed.

"Touch and go," the doctor said. "He's lost a lot of blood, and he has some broken bones. The bones in one leg have been crushed. He's had a concussion and is in an induced coma. But at least he doesn't have a fractured skull."

"At least that's something," Ernie said.

"And what's surprising," the doctor added, "is that his bones are unusually heavy in his skull and through his body. So the effects of the accident aren't as bad as they could be."

"Do you know what happened?" Ernie asked.

"Well, according to the police, a car hit him, knocked him under the car, and ran over his leg. So we're doing what we can," the doctor concluded. "We have surgery scheduled for tomorrow to set the bones and drain any fluids from the inflammation that occurs after any serious injury."

"You'll keep us informed?" Ernie asked.

"Of course," the doctor said.

Then, he rushed off to see another patient in the ICU. Ernie and Maggie walked out of the ICU and down the corridor.

"I guess we can't do anything more here," Ernie said.

"No, we can't. And we should get back to make sure all the other kids are all right. I'm sure the care workers will want to go home for tonight."

"Right," Ernie agreed.

A few minutes later, they were in their car heading home.

"At least we haven't had any calls from the media," Ernie commented.

"No, thank God for that. They probably think this is another routine car accident," Maggie said.

"Let's only hope."

Ernie pulled into the driveway, and they went inside the house, where all the kids were asleep in their beds.

Alonso and Vanessa, the two care workers, greeted them at the door, and smiled happily when Ernie told them, "You can go home now. We're back."

After they left, Ernie and Maggie settled back on the living room couch, relieved to be home. Then, Ernie got up, grabbed a bottle of wine from the cabinet above the sink, and poured a glass of wine for each of them.

"Until tomorrow," he said as he brought the glasses over to the coffee table in front of the couch.

"Yeah, till then," Maggie said, as she picked up her glass. "And all my thoughts and prayers are with Joey."

"My thoughts and prayers, too," said Ernie. "And for the doctors. Here's hoping they can bring Joey back."

They continued to drink their wine in silence, thinking of Joey surrounded by a tangle of tubes and wires and covered by a stark white sheet, as he lay unconscious to the world.

CHAPTER 8: THE AFTERMATH

The next day as Ernie and Maggie headed to their car in the garage, a reporter and cameraman jumped in front of them.

"Are you going to see the boy?" the reporter asked, while the cameraman began filming.

"What's this?" Ernie said angrily.

"Who sent you here?" Maggie asked.

As they spoke, a news van pulled up on the street and then another.

"Are you crazy?" Ernie said, trying to push past the reporter, who stepped ahead of Ernie and blocked his way.

"How dare you?" Ernie screamed at him.

"We can write this story without you. We'd just like a comment from you," the reporter said.

"From me?" Ernie was even angrier.

"What story? Why are you here?" Maggie said, as she saw the reporters and cameramen emerging from the three vans parked on the street.

"Because someone at the hospital told us about the accident and the boy in the ICU."

"But that's confidential," Ernie sputtered.

"Not always," the reporter said. "When there's a big story. we have our sources."

"Big story! What do you mean?" Ernie said.

"Because it's a Neanderthal boy," said the reporter. "Supposedly they died out many thousands of years ago. But now they're back."

"Jesus!" Ernie exclaimed.

He looked around desperately, and Maggie grabbed his hand tightly, as if grabbing a lifeline.

At the same time, the three reporters and three camerapersons from the van were closing in, about to confront him with their notebooks and cameras. Ernie felt like he was about to be encircled and trapped.

"Look, can't you leave us alone?" Maggie begged. "We don't know anything else other than that the boy's in the hospital and fighting for his life."

The reporters scrawled furiously.

"Fighting for his life, you say?" said one of the reporters. He turned to the cameraman beside him. "You got that, didn't you?"

The cameraman nodded, as he continued pointing his camera at Ernie.

"What did they tell you about his injuries?" said the first reporter.

"And what are his chances," the second reporter said.

"Damn you. Damn you all to hell," Ernie screamed at them.

"Please. Please," Maggie begged. "Let us go. Have a heart. We don't know more and have to get to the hospital. Don't any of you have any family members who got hurt?"

Again, the reporters scrawled furiously and the cameras whirred.

"You consider the boy a family member?" the third reporter called out.

Maggie and Ernie ignored him.

"Just let us go," she begged again. "We don't have any more to say now."

This time the reporters and camera people let them through. They separated, half of the reporters and camera people on one side, half on the other, like the parting of the Red Sea. Ernie and Maggie hurried to their car, as the camera people ran after them and filmed, as Ernie opened the garage door with the remote, and he and Maggie quickly got in the car.

As Ernie roared out of the driveway, the reporters and cameramen scurried out of the way and took their last shots of the car barreling down the street. After that, they rushed to their cars and vans to follow Ernie and Maggie to the hospital, hoping to find the answers to their questions there.

* * * * * *

A few minutes later, Ernie and Maggie stood in the corridor with Dr. Matt Perez outside Joey's private room.

"We moved him here," Dr. Perez explained, "since we're not doing anymore procedures. So now it's just 'Wait and see.'"

Dr. Perez led them into the room where Dannie was lying with all kinds of tubes and wires extending from his head and body. They were connected to machines that were blipping out graphs and numbers which showed that Joey was still breathing and getting fluids and nutrition internally.

"What do you think, doctor?" Ernie asked.

"We've seen a little improvement, but we're keeping him in an induced coma for another day or two. And the nurses and doctors are checking him regularly."

Ernie and Maggie watched silently for another minute, until Dr. Perez broke the silence.

"Well, we better go outside now. We'll let you know if anything changes."

"Can you let us know either way?" Maggie asked.

"Yes," Dr. Perez said.

"What about the news media?" Ernie said when they were back in the corridor, the door to Joey's room closed behind them. "How did they know about this?"

Ernie and Maggie glanced down the corridor, relieved to see only doctors, nurses, and orderlies walking about.

"I don't know," Dr. Perez replied. "No one from the hospital staff officially said anything. The media must have learned about this from someone working here who found out and leaked the news. The hospital staff will investigate and try to find out."

"So what do we do?" Maggie asked.

"You don't have to do anything more now. And we'll keep you informed," Dr. Perez assured them.

"Okay. Thank you," Ernie said.

Then, at the door leaving the hospital, Ernie and Maggie were mobbed by a rush of reporters and camera persons, even larger than before. They shielded their eyes from the bright lights of reflectors shining at them.

"How is he?" one reporter shouted out.

"Is he still alive?" said another.

"What do the doctors say?" said a third.

Ernie and Maggie said nothing. They just pushed their way through the crowd, and several reporters moved back to let them through.

Then, like a pack of wolves, the reporters and camera persons chased them to their car in the hospital parking lot.

At last, Ernie and Maggie slammed the doors and Ernie backed up, as a few reporters tapped on the windows and the cameras rolled.

"They're like bees; a swarm of bees," Ernie said to Maggie.

"Just trying to sting," Maggie added.

Then, as Ernie backed into the main lane of the parking lot, the reporters and camera persons spread out to give them room. Ernie stepped on the gas, free at last.

"At least that's over with," Ernie commented, as they drove on the freeway towards home.

"At least until tomorrow," Maggie observed.

But that night, as they watched the news on TV, after the kids in the group home were asleep, they realized it wasn't over at all.

Suddenly, after the national news and a commercial break, the screen showed the reporters and camera persons confronting them at their front door and as they entered and left the hospital.

"And now this breaking story," the news anchor said. "We have just learned that a boy who was hit by a car and is in the hospital fighting for his life is a Neanderthal boy. And that has raised the big questions. 'Are the Neanderthals still alive? And how did he end up in the hospital?' All our thoughts and prayers are with this poor boy to survive. But we have so many questions. So many questions."

Ernie clicked the remote off and slammed it down.

"Crap! Crap! And double crap!" he yelled. "They know! They know!"

"And they'll be here with questions tomorrow," Maggie said, worriedly grabbing Ernie's hand.

"I know. And this is just the beginning of the media nightmare."

"My God! What do we do? And what about all the other Neanderthal kids who are here? I thought we could raise them quietly like the other special needs kids."

"And now we can't. It'll be a media circus," Ernie said.

Ernie staggered up from the couch

"So what can we do?" Maggie said, her voice cracking with anguish.

"I don't know. But I'm going to call our lawyer and tell Darryl and Jeremy what's going on. Maybe they'll know what to do."

Ernie picked up the phone on the table by the couch.

Moments later, his lawyer, Carl Johnson, was on the phone.

"Carl, we have a serious problem," said Ernie. "I need you to tell us what to do."

CHAPTER 9: WHAT'S NEXT?

A few weeks later, Ernie and Maggie were back from the hospital with Joey, who was still very weak and disoriented but on the mend. To get home, they drove through the ever-present throng of journalists who surrounded their car before they could get into the garage, after Ernie opened the door with the remote.

"We heard Joey is home now. How's he doing?" yelled one reporter, sticking a microphone in Ernie's face.

"Will Joey be able to talk to us?" said another, tapping on the window next to Maggie.

"Who's the scientist who brought the Neanderthal's back?" a third reporter called out.

Ernie and Maggie looked straight ahead and tried to ignore them, while Ernie stepped slowly on the gas to move ahead. As he inched forward, several reporters and camera people stepped aside.

Meanwhile, in the back of the car, his leg stretched out in a cast, Joey turned this way and that to see what was going on. He was fascinated to see the people outside of the car holding long handles with bulbs on them, while others dangled big black boxes with long necks from their shoulders. The people seemed so excited and eager that they made him tingle with excitement, too. Maybe they might be fun to play with, Joey thought, like the little metal soldiers he lined up to battle against each other. Suddenly, some of them were shouting loudly and reaching to the car like they wanted something and would fight hard to get it. But inside the car, he felt protected from all that. Then, when he heard the roar of the engine, as Ernie inched forward, he felt very powerful, like these were people to rule over or animals to kill. For now, as he looked down at his outstretched foot in a cast, he couldn't do very much. If only he was strong like the warriors he played with or the soldiers and boxes he saw fighting on TV.

At last, Ernie pulled into the garage and clicked on the remote to shut the garage door. He and Maggie carefully lifted Joey into the fold-up wheelchair they unfolded. They carefully secured him with straps, his leg stretched out ahead of him, and placed a blanket over him to keep him warm. Then, they wheeled him through the side door into the kitchen.

So they were back! Moments later, the two home care assistants and the five other Neanderthal kids rushed forward to welcome them back. The three Down Syndrome kids lingered in the background, a little stunned by all the commotion.

"Welcome back," one of the home care assistants said.

"What can we do to help?" said the other.

"Just take Joey to his room and make him comfortable," Maggie said.

"No bed," Joey said.

"Okay. You can sit up," Ernie told him. "Whatever you're comfortable doing."

"But you need plenty of rest," Maggie said. "You have a lot to heal."

Then, as the home care assistants took Joey to his room, Ernie and Maggie looked through the shuttered blinds to see if the media was still there.

And they were, waiting like jackals in the bush, ready to pounce on their weakened prey.

* * * * * * *

Meanwhile, Joey was delighted to be back in his room with Davy and Bobby. He pulled the blanket to show off his leg in a cast.

"Look," he said. "From the hospital."

He pointed to a few signatures scrawled on his cast.

"The people there wrote these. 'So you remember us,' they said."

Davy grabbed a pen from the small desk by the window.

"Oh, wow! I can write my name, too."

"Write name?" Joey asked.

"Yes. Miss Duncan showed me how."

Moments later, Davy scribbled his name on the cast.

"Me, too," said Bobby, and he added his name.

Then, Joey was curious to look outside. He wheeled over to the window, pushed apart two of the shutters, and peeped out.

"People!" he exclaimed. "Lots of people. With big boxes and long handles. Like around our car."

"Oowee!" said Davy, "I want to see, too."

Then he looked out the window.

Meanwhile, in the backyard, several reporters furiously took notes, while two video and single shot cameras snapped away.

As they did, Ernie and Maggie saw the mad rush of another half-dozen reporters and camera people to the backyard.

"My God!" Ernie called out. "They're going to Joey's room."

Ernie rushed through the house, Maggie just behind him.

As they came into the room, they saw Joey and Davy smiling and waving at the window.

"Oh my God, no!" Maggie shrieked.

Ernie quickly ran over to Joey and pulled him away from the window, while Maggie grabbed and Davy away.

"You can't look out the window!" Ernie said.

"But they smiled and waved at us," Joey said.

"No, no. You don't understand. They can't see you."

"But they saw us! They waved. They friendly."

"And they take our pictures," said Davy.

"Well, you can't do that anymore," Ernie said, realizing that it would be difficult to explain to Joey, Davy, and Bobby or the other Neanderthal children why they couldn't do this.

Ernie reached up and quickly closed the shutters, and he told the home care assistants, who had come into the room, "You have to keep the children away from the windows. You have to keep the shutters closed. You can't let anyone see them."

But now, as much as Ernie and Maggie might want to shut the children away from the world, it was already too late. As they both realized, the reporters already had their notes and the camera people already had their pictures.

"So what can we do?" Maggie asked, as they left the boys' room, leaving the home care assistants behind to calm the boys down.

"I don't know," said Ernie, shutting the door behind them. "That'll be one more thing to ask our lawyer Carl, when he comes over in a little while."

Back in the kitchen, Maggie poured two cups of coffee and handed one to Ernie.

"Let's just chill out for a while. There's not much more we can do while we wait for Carl."

Ernie nodded and they sank down on the living room couch. As they quietly drank their coffee, Ernie clicked on the remote to watch the news. It was almost a relief to see the crisis playing out around the world. It made their own struggle with the media seem that much smaller and less important.

"At least we can be thankful that Joey's getting better," Ernie said to Maggie.

"Yes, thank God he's going to be okay, and the doctor says we can expect a full recovery."

So they settled back, calm now, as they watched jets and bombs flying over Syria, water flooding after hurricanes in Florida, and the President announcing yet another planned military strike in the Middle East.

Then, the local news came on, and this time the anchor led off with photos of Joey and Davy peering and waving through the window.

"Oh, no!" Maggie gasped.

Then, the two news anchors, Rhett Andrews and Sue Winston, began talking about the photos.

"That's quite a story, isn't it," said Rhett. "A local kid got hit by a car and just came back from the hospital."

"So he's going to be okay," said Sue.

"Yes, but that's not the big story," Rhett continued. "It turns out he's a Neanderthal boy, and so is the other boy at the window with him. So that raises the question. How did the kids get here? Are the Neanderthals back, and how?"

"That's right, and we already have some questions from our listeners," Sue noted, raising a handful of sheets of paper from the studio ticker tape. "Here's one. The viewer asks if the Neanderthals are really humans. Or are they more like apes?"

"That's a good one. I don't know."

"And here's another," said Sue, glancing at another piece of paper. "This viewer wants to know: 'What will happen if there's an insurance claim? Will the boy be treated like a child or like a pet who got hurt? And how will the insurance company determine fault? Did the kid just run out in the street so he's at fault? Or did the driver not see him, since it was getting dark, though he should have seen him if he had his lights on?"

"Wow! Now there's a lawyer or lawyer in the making who's wondering about this."

"Or maybe an insurance agent," suggested Sue. "Anyway, this story is sure one that'll get us thinking. And you know this is a story that'll go national. Even international. It'll be a big story everywhere."

"Meanwhile, the authorities are still looking for the driver of the car," Rhett added. "And now a word from our sponsor."

Ernie angrily clicked off the TV.

"God damn it! I can't believe this. We just got Joey back from the hospital, and already people are talking about his legal status and whether he's a real person."

Maggie grabbed his hand to soothe him. "I know. It's terrible what the media can do. But we've got to be strong, at least for Joey's sake and for the other kids."

"I know. I know. But how? What do we say? What do we do?"

Just then, the doorbell rang, sounding like the loud gong announcing the end of a round at a fight.

"At least that should be Carl," Ernie said. "Hopefully, he can tell us what to do."

A few minutes later, Carl, a 40something lawyer specializing in torts and litigation, was sitting across from Ernie and Maggie in the living room.

Ernie quickly explained what had happened, ending with the plaint: "So now the story of Joey and the Neanderthal kids is about to go worldwide, and we're in the middle of this."

"And so are Darryl and Jeremy created these kids in the first place," Carl said. "Plus I imagine the lab where they worked and any surrogate mother or assistants who worked on creating these kids will be involved, too."

"Oh, my, God," said Ernie. "I never thought...We just wanted to help out by giving these kids a good home."

"And so you have. But you have to realize, these are not just like special needs kids with a disability. These kids raise all kinds of questions about what it means to be human and what kind of rights these kids and their creators or guardians have."

"We didn't know," Maggie said weakly.

"I know. But this is likely to be the beginning of a long legal fight, and you better believe me, politicians will get involved. There will be legislators, government officials, and politicians on both sides of the aisle with different points of view. It'll be like the fight over LGBTQ rights and what kind of status and rights they have in society."

"Jesus!" said Ernie.

"And if Darryl and Jeremy were able to create these kids from ancient DNA, that means other scientists might be able to do this, too. So there soon could be more Neanderthal kids elsewhere around the country, around the world. It's likely the scientists and their backers may try to keep all of this quiet at first. But then, almost certainly, the word will get out, because once a scientific or technological breakthrough is successful, others will try to repeat it."

"But legally…" Ernie began.

"Damn the law! To these innovators, the law won't matter, and the law is always playing catch up anyway, when there is a major new technology or scientific breakthrough that changes everything in society."

"You think this will?" Ernie asked.

"Of course I do," Carl said. "So you better be prepared. And I will, too, when the legal suits begin about the accident and about creating and raising these kids in the first place. I'll also be here for you when the media comes calling, and I can speak for you and Joey and the other kids. Or I can help you know what to say."

"Thank you. I don't know what to do next," said Ernie.

"Well, just get prepared. It's going to be a long bumpy ride. It's like being in the Wild West discovering a new frontier. I think the first step is to circle the wagons, and then we'll figure out what we and everyone else involved with these kids needs to do to have a successful ride to get through this mess."

PART II: THE NEW NEANDERTHALS POLICE FORCE

CHAPTER 10: CREATING THE FORCE

When John Montgomery, the head of the Robot Works Factory, read about the work of Darryl Jonas with Neanderthals he was intrigued. The newspaper story said that Jonas had secretly created six Neanderthal kids and raised them in a lab before placing them in a group home, where they lived quietly before the media discovered them.

"How clever," he thought. "Bring the kids back and raise them like ordinary kids in modern society.

He put down the newspaper with the blaring headlines about how one of the kids went exploring and was hit by a car, after which the cops and the media arrived.

Montgomery turned to his associate, Dan Hunter, the Research Director.

"Tough luck," he said. "Now the kids will grow up in the spotlight, unless Jonas can figure out some way to keep them away, so the kids can live ordinary lives."

"Yes, so sad," Dan agreed.

"But what if...."

John was thinking now, speculating on what this discovery of Neanderthal kids, created by cloning, could mean for the future of science and technology. He looked out from his window overseeing operations where rows of precision machines turned out an army of robots to work in retail stores and factories. With a flip of a switch or the click of a few buttons on a remote, the robots could file out along the store or factory floor and do any of the simple tasks they had been programmed to do. They could select the correct items from a shelf and put them in a bin to be packaged and shipped to a customer. They could load and unload trucks with supplies or completed projects. They could stand by a conveyer belt and put in selected parts. They could even go out in the fields and plant crops or pull fruit from trees.

He mentally clicked through the many tasks the robots could do. But each simple task required many hours of software development and programming to train the robot to do a particular tasks. Then, if something changed, such as the size of a product going through the conveyor belt or the slope of a field after a heavy rain, the robot had to be programmed again. Yet it was still cheaper than hiring workers at a minimum wage that kept going up and up.

But what if...What if? He imagined there could be dozens of Neanderthals raised and bred to perform such tasks. Then, since Neanderthals were supposed to be strong with relatively low IQs, maybe they would be ideally suited to perform such tasks with no need to pay them.

And what else? What else?

He kept on thinking of the possibilities, as well as the chance to make his own scientific achievement by creating a team of Neanderthal workers.

Just then, Dan Hunter interrupted his thoughts.

"Hey, boss. You've been so quiet and staring into space for a few minutes. What's up?"

John jerked back to the present. He handed the newspaper to Dan and pointed to the headline.

"I was just thinking about how we could do this, too. We could bring someone to get some Neanderthal DNA for us and raise some Neanderthal kids ourselves."

"That sound pretty complicated," Dan said.

"Well, then, how about this. Now that the secret to creating Neanderthals is out, maybe we could get some Neanderthal kids created and raised by other companies. Then, when they're about seven, we could start training them, and maybe they could start doing some work for us on the assembly line."

"What about hiring them out to work for others?" Dan suggested.

"That, too," John said. "We could create teams of Neanderthal workers and rent them out or sell them. You never know what can happen."

"But how do we get that the kids?" Dan asked.

"Look, I know people who know people. You don't ask a lot of questions, and if you've got the money they get it done. They can take care of the kids in their early years. You know, find some mothers, teachers, care facilities, sports trainers, whatever they need to do to bring them up. Then, they turn the kids over to us when they're old enough to work, and we take it from there."

And so the seed was planted. John and Dan began exploring the possibility of developing a team of Neanderthal workers to work with and eventually replace their robots. The possibilities seemed endless, as John and Dan thought about all the things they might train their Neanderthals to do.

A few weeks later, John met with Anthony, who was known as a fixer around town.

"Just tell me what you need, and if the price is right, I'll get it for you," Anthony said, as he sat across from John in his office. "What do you need?"

John explained about his idea of creating a workforce with Neanderthals."

"They're so strong and powerful," John said. "I thought with a little training, they could do routine tasks better and more cheaply than robots. They don't need a lot of programming to get them to perform a task. Just show and tell, and they can do it. And they can better adapt to changes in procedures. Just a little explanation, no need for new programming and it's done."

"A good idea, sir," said Anthony.

"So can you do it?"

"Sure. We know of some individuals and companies in California, the South, and Mexico who have started to create Neanderthal babies and raise them in the first years of life."

"But how?

"No more questions. They learned about the new DNA technology for creating Neanderthals and figured it will become a new business So they're gearing up to create the kids.

"Secretly?"

"Of course. They'll be raising them out in the country or in another country, This is just the beginning, and this is gonna be a new business that's gonna be huge. But don't worry. I'll be your liaison and get all the kids you need when they're about seven years old and ready to go to work. I can also arrange for you to visit from time to time while they are growing up."

John smiled. "Sounds good. How much and where do I sign."

Anthony brought out several pages of documents. "Say, $25,000 now to place your order for 50 kids at $1000 a kid, with the other $25,000 due when we bring you the kids."

"That's fine," said John, and he signed the agreement.

Anthony put the papers back in his briefcase. "And if this goes well...."

"Yes, there could be many more orders. And maybe we can even act as your agent for creating many more teams around the country."

"You've to it," said Anthony as he reached over to shake hands. "Just think it could be the beginning of Neanderthal Enterprises."

"Yes, it could," John said, imagining all of the money that creating teams of Neanderthals for his own company and other companies could bring."

* * * * * * *

But after he returned from one of his trips to see how the Neanderthals, now three, were doing, he felt he could lose it all. He had been on a plane trip returning home, and he got a little tipsy from the drinks served on the plane. Then, he talked too

80

much to the man sitting beside him, a scientist who taught biology at a university and did experiments at a lab.

"Well, we've got an experiment to beat all experiments," John said. "It's a project that can change the world."

Then, he bragged about how his company had arranged the cloning and how he had hired a man he knew who could get things done to create a workforce of Neanderthals.

"In a few more years they'll be ready. And maybe you could use your own team of Neanderthals to help you -- maybe work as assistants in your lab or be subjects for your experiments."

"Sure, maybe. Can I have your card," the man said, and John imagined everything was fine. Maybe a client for Neanderthal Enterprises down the road.

But a few days later, he got a call from his foreman supervising the robots on the factory floor.

"It's Jackie Willis. She said that she has some important information that will concern you," the foreman said.

"Yeah, sure. Send her up," John said, figuring it was one more company rep trying to sell him some supplies or maybe hire his company to do some packing and shipping for them.

A few minutes later, Jackie was seated across from him in his office.

"So what can I do for you?" John smiled pleasantly.

"Well, it's about your Neanderthal project," Jackie said.

"What? How do you know?" John asked. He could feel his jaw tightening, his body starting to quiver with anxiety as he spoke.

"My friend who was on a plane with you. You told him all about it and gave him your card.'

John's mind raced back to that conversation on the plane. What was he thinking? How could he talk about the project, much less give the man his card?

"Uhhh... I was a little tipsy on the ride. I shouldn't have said anything."

Jackie looked at him sternly. "Well, now you have, and we know what you are doing, and we don't approve."

John tensed even more. "What? Who's we?"

"I belong to a small group of human rights advocates, and we're in touch with other human rights groups."

"Huhhh?"

"Well, let me put it this way. We monitor the way poor and exploited people are treated, like immigrant families that are broken up or kids put in cages. Then, if people are being mistreated, we let the media know. We contact government officials about passing laws."

John's nervously gave way to anger.

"Jesus! Look, we're not mistreating anyone," he said with increasing firmness. "The people raising the kids are treating them like normal kids, and then we'll be treating them like regular workers in a factory, with breaks for lunch, coffee, time off to be with their families. This isn't going to be like some slave camp"

"Then, why the secrecy? If they're not being treated right, we could..."

"Look. The kids are already three years old. Do you really want to expose them to that? It'd be circus. The kids' lives would be ruined. They'd be treated like animals in a zoo. But with us they've got a future. We have people teaching them. They'll become workers. They'll get money. A chance to live happy lives with other workers."

Jackie looked thoughtful, then finally replied.

"That all sounds very nice. But do you really expect me to believe you?"

"Yes, I do."

"But those are just fine words. What's to keep you from just doing what you want; exploiting them when they go to work so it's like a chain gang? Or like a new form of slavery?"

"Well, it won't be. Besides, you already know about us. Others can find out about us. So we'd have to treat them right or get called out if we didn't, wouldn't we?"

"Yes."

"Besides, the DNA technology for creating new generations of Neanderthals is already out of the bag. There are individuals and companies all over the world raising Neanderthals, and after a while the thousands of Neanderthals will grow up and start having kids."

"I know. So we're doing what we can to see that the Neanderthals are treated well and they don't become an exploited underclass that's treated like many immigrants and minority group members. And if we see you start doing that..."

"Well, we won't. So all I ask of you is to not say anything about this to others. Don't contact the media. Don't spread this on the social media. Don't turn this into a circus."

"Okay. I guess we could do that. But know that we'll be watching. We'll check what you're doing. And if the Neanderthals have any problem, we'll be ready to act and do something."

"Then, we have an understanding."

"Yes, agreed. But you have our warning."

"Sure, I understand."

Jackie got up, turned, and left his office.

John sighed, relieved to see her go, though afraid of what might happen should she and her group disagree with anything they were doing and decide to alert the media, which would also let competitors know and start their own Neanderthal projects.

But at least for now, he felt he had pushed aside the potential threat. Yet, what of the future? He wasn't sure, but he still felt worried about the potential harm that Jackie and her group might cause.

CHAPTER 11: WORK IT

After the Neanderthals were seven, John thought they might be ready to start working. Alice Miller, who had been teaching them for Anthony, indicated they could understand basic commands and speak simple sentences. So John called together Dan Hunter and his top managers in the factory into the conference room to explain what they could do.

"Alice is a member of the team of teachers who have been helping the Neanderthals develop basic language and everyday living skills. The teachers are adapting what they teach based on what we know about the behavior and cognitive development of the Neanderthals many thousands of years ago."

"That's right," said Alice. "We know they must have been able to communicate basic information to organize a hunt. And scientists have discovered that they had a hyoid bone, a horseshoe-shaped structure in the throat, like modern humans. So we presume they could speak and had language. The Neanderthals are also believed to be the first cave artists, with some very simple cave art in Cantabria Spain, dating back to about 65,000 years ago, a time before modern humans appeared in Europe around 40,000-45,000 years ago. But it's very simple, only very rough outlines of animals and humans." She projected a slide from her computer on the screen.

"That cave art suggests the Neanderthals had some abilities to think symbolically, but not at the level of modern humans. So that's how we've been teaching the Neanderthal kids -- as if they might have the cognitive abilities of five or six years old."

"But what if they were taught as if they could learn even more?" Dan asked.

"We don't know," John replied. "And we haven't tried, since we are basically raising the Neanderthals based on their ability to be very strong and aggressive, as well as communicate enough to be on teams. That's what our investors are interested in -- creating teams of Neanderthals to replace expensive robots powered by artificial intelligence or AI. The robots can become very expensive as the programming becomes more complex. If we can raise the Neanderthals to do this work instead, that's a big advantage."

"Understood," Dan agreed.

"So let Alice continue to explain when we can start having the kids work for us."

Alice flipped to another slide showing a recreation of a traditional Neanderthal family.

"According to the researchers, it would appear that the children grew up at about the same rate as modern humans, since they had a life span of about 50 years. At about 7 years old, the Neanderthal child might be physically the equivalent to a human child. Yet based on their lack of any written language and their very simple art, we've been estimating that they would have the ability of a five to six year old child."

"But what about their larger brain size," Dan wondered.

"It doesn't matter," said Alice. "It's how the neurons are connected together. Researchers believe the Neanderthals dedicated more of their brains to controlling their bodies, since they were stockier and stronger, and their larger, stronger bodies required more brain control. The Neanderthals also dedicated more of their brain power to vision than modern humans, since the larger eye sockets in their skeletons indicate they had a larger visual cortex than us."

"It's like the circuitry in a computer," Dan commented. "After all, the first computers were very huge, almost the size of a large room. Now the parts are smaller than ever, even microscopic."

"Exactly," said Alice. "That's why we're suggesting that the Neanderthal kids could begin working as young as seven years old. In fact, there are many examples of young kids starting to work and train, such as in family stores and farms, where kids start helping out. Researchers estimate that at seven, the Neanderthals' brain size was about 88% that of an adult compared to the modern human brain size at seven, which is about 95% that of an adult."

"Meaning?" Dan asked.

"Meaning that by seven their brain was pretty much developed, so they could do most of the tasks of an adult, adjusting for their smaller size, of course."

"And that means," John said, "we can easily start putting these kids to work. We can take advantage of their qualities where they are better than humans -- such as their greater strength, aggressiveness, and visual ability. Plus they can work in small groups, and they have some basic communication and language skills, so we can readily teach them what to do. Then, we can use them as best suited to their level of skills and abilities."

And so it was decided. The Neanderthal kids would continue to live in the small group home that was set up for them. It had already been divided into sections corresponding to the work teams of 8 to 12 Neanderthals.

John thought these arrangements ideal, because in the past few years, the Neanderthals had spent several hours a day with Alice, learning some basic words and sentences, so they could understand simple instructions and talk to each other. Occasionally, she had invited them to experiment with using brushes and paints to draw simple outlines and shapes, such as appeared in the early cave art by Neanderthals or early humans.

Then, too, they had had a chance to play in the grassy backyard behind the lab, which had high walls so no one driving by could see them. Mostly their play consisted of running around, playing tag and hide and seek, throwing balls, and jumping up and down, much like dogs and cats might play with each other. They had sometimes used plastic or foam spears and hammers as if they were back in the woods hunting down bears and mammoths. And sometimes John had let in some chickens or wild game for them to chase, after which the Neanderthals and staff members had enjoyed cooking the meat for dinner over a campfire.

As John explained when the experiment started: "I want to recreate Neanderthal times as much as possible while the kids are growing up."

But now it was time to continue the experiment and put the kids to work. John had high hopes of the possibility.

As he and Dan led Alice out of the conference room, he commented: "I think we're really onto something here. It'll be a real breakthrough. Just think. If we can show that the

Neanderthal kids make great workers, we can raise more and more kids and have Neanderthal teams working everywhere. It'll be a whole new workforce for the 21st century -- and we were the first to come up with the idea."

CHAPTER 12: THE BIG PAYOFF

Ten years later, John Montgomery stood with Dan Hunter in their shipping department watching the Neanderthals work. At one time, the company had nearly a hundred robots scurrying from shelf to shelf picking up packages. As needed, their team of AI specialists repeatedly changed the programming, so the robots would go to different shelves or pick up more than one package for multiple orders. At times, the specialists fixed the circuitry when robots somehow collided with each other.

As John commented to Dan as they watched: "Just think how much we are saving now. The transition really works. Before we not only had the cost of creating the robots, but then we had the cost of the programmers programming them. And if things went wrong, the AI guys had to program the robots again."

"That's right," Dan agreed. "And don't forget the replacement costs when robots crashed into each other and couldn't be fixed. Or the costs of replacing merchandise, when the programming went haywire and the robots knocked over some shelves."

"I know. But the Neanderthals are so much more careful. And they know to pick up things and put them back."

"They don't crash into each other either."

"No they don't. They're definitely more cost effective. And I like their strength. You don't have to worry about them breaking under too much weight, since they bring in another Neanderthal or two to help them lift or move things. Like a real team."

"You can't program the robots to do that."

"No," said John, his cheek swelling with pride. "The Neanderthals are a great team. And they're our team."

John and Dan fell silent as they continued watching the Neanderthal team in action.

A few minutes later, the 5 p.m. whistle blew and the Neanderthals working on the floor stopped and filed out, while another Neanderthal team filed in. Soon they had scattered around the warehouse and began working. John turned proudly back to Dan.

"Sure, we need two or three teams for shifts, so the Neanderthals can get some sleep and have some time off to be with their friends, like they're a family. So they need some break times, while the robots can work continuously for days or weeks until their circuitry gets too hot and they have to cool down."

"Or they crash and break down," Dan added.

"Yes, that, too," said John. "But even with all the food and meal breaks, the Neanderthals still are more cost effective, since we don't have to pay them. Just keep them fit and healthy, so they can stay well and strong."

John beamed as he looked down on the shipping floor.

"They've been doing a great job in our factory, too."

As John talked, another team of Neanderthals were working in the factory, where they pulled parts off an assembly line and put them together to create a mechanical toy.

"So you might say they're the perfect work force. They take direction well and seem to learn quickly. Then, they do whatever we ask them to do."

"Or what others ask of them."

"Of course. We just have to introduce them to their new leader and train them to do what he or she wants. So now, if we can just keep our work with them secret for a little longer, we can continue to get new accounts without any competition. Let's let everyone think we are just creating robots for them, and we should do fine."

Just then John's secretary called on his mobile phone.

"The company interested in your robots is here," she said.

"Good. Dan and I will be right down," John said.

He clicked the phone off and turned to Dan.

"Our meeting. Is all the paperwork in order?"

Dan nodded and they went down the corridor to the main building.

The client, Stan Bigelow, and two associates, Frank and Rick, were already seated in the conference room. Dan pulled out three agreement forms and handed them to Stan and his associates.

"What's this?" Stan asked.

"An NDA," John said. "You need to sign it before we discuss anything."

"But why? We're just here to get some robots for our factory. Nothing secret about that. You advertise them everywhere, promote them at trade shows."

"Yes, but you wanted to know how you can save money with our newer robot program. And we have something top secret to show you."

Stan glared down at the contract, jumped up, and glared at John angrily.

"But it says we could be liable for millions of dollars if we share what you tell us. That's highway robbery."

"Not if you don't say anything," said John. "We just want to make sure our project stays secret until we are ready to announce this to the world. So we only show it selectively to certain handpicked clients or referrals."

Stan relaxed and sat back down. He looked at the agreement again.

"But you haven't shown me anything yet. Am I obligated to get it if I don't like it."

"No, not at all. Just be quiet about anything we show you. Don't tell anyone. Not even your wife or kids. This secret has to remain confidential, so it's only known to those invited into this room for our special presentation and to everyone working on this project"

"That's right," said Dan firmly. "This has been our company's trade secret for 10 years, and we intend to keep it that way."

"Okay, okay," said Stan, signing reluctantly.

He passed the agreement to his two associates who signed, too. Then, he passed their signed agreement to John.

"All right," said John scooping up the agreements. "Let's begin, and I'll show you what our big secret program is all about."

A few minutes later, John, Dan, Stan and his associates were in the small control center overlooking the warehouse.

"This is it," said John, pointing to the warehouse floor, where a few dozen Neanderthals were rushing back and forth picking up boxes from the shelves and filling them up with different items for shipment."

"But those aren't robots," Stan exclaimed. "You have people working on the shelves."

"No. Not ordinary people," John replied. "They're Neanderthals. And it turns out they're cheaper and more efficient than humans or robots. Now you can have them working for you, too, as long as you see the value and keep who you hire secret."

"Or lose millions if you sue us," said Stan grimly.

"No. Make millions if you work with us," John countered. "So are you in? Do you want a team of Neanderthals working with you in your factory? We'll provide the training and instructions for dealing with the Neanderthals. We'll tell you everything you need to be successful, and within a few weeks you'll see how your costs go down and your profits go up."

"It's a win-win solution for you," said Dan.

"You just have to keep it secret," said John.

Stan reached out his hand.

"Okay. A deal. I'll pay you for each Neanderthal worker, take care of them, and put them to work like you say. And like you say, I'll keep the project secret."

John extended his hand and shook hands with Stan.

"Very good. We have a deal."

Then, John, Dan, Stan, and his associates looked down at the shipping warehouse, as the Neanderthal workers continued to walk or run around quickly to find the right items, fill up packages, and put them on the conveyer belt.

"And look over there. As you can see for yourself," said John, "they continue to work so quickly and do their tasks with a kind of military precision. Now, you'll have them doing that for you, too."

"Yeah, that's what I like about this," Stan commented. "Having a great team to work for us. Thanks for letting us in on your secret operation. And if this works well, we'll want to order many more. Yes, many, many more."

CHAPTER 13: CREATING EVEN MORE NEANDERTHALS

After Stan and his associates left, John smiled broadly at Dan, who was sitting nearby.

"Well, we did it," John exclaimed. "Our biggest contract yet. One million. And we can expand even more if we can clone and breed our Neanderthal workers quickly enough."

"I'll check into it," said Dan, "and I'll look for a few more barracks or warehouses we can set up with beds. Anthony is working on getting the DNA for us from different burial sites. And they're willing to give up some DNA for research purposes."

"Wonderful. It's a good thing we set up that non-profit foundation for DNA research."

"Yes," said Dan. "For medical and health improvements."

"Exactly. And that's true. Nobody needs to know how we're using the discoveries to create a Neanderthal workforce."

"And they won't," said Dan. "Not even our security guards, administrators, or medical staff know what this is all about."

"Good. And at least Jackie and her group have been off our case for a while, since they've been focusing on sex trafficking and foreign workers subjected to inhumane conditions."

John gazed around his office with photos of the Neanderthals at work, as he continued. "We've been able to do this for ten years, so now we just need to keep doing what we've been doing. Then, everything should work out fine."

John pulled out a bottle of wine from a cabinet on the wall.

"So let's celebrate," he said, popping the cork.

He poured two glasses of wine and gave one to Dan.

"To continued success in spreading the Neanderthal work teams everywhere."

Dan laughed. "Yeah. To success. It'll be like the way they spread around Europe and Asia thousands of years ago."

"Right," said John holding his glass up high. "But now they aren't just spreading as they follow and hunt their game. Instead, it's a whole new game, and we're in charge and winning the game."

John and Dan clicked their glasses together and laughed as they raised them to their lips and savored the wine.

After that, Dan went downstairs to check over operations. Everything seemed to be running so smoothly. The conveyor belts were running by quickly with packages. The Neanderthals were going around as they had been instructed to find packages with colored dots that represented numbers for different items. He was pleased they had even learned to identify a series of 8 to 12 numbers, so they could distinguish different items and place the correct ones in a large package for shipping.

He also noticed their agility in climbing ladders to reach items on the higher shelves, while the robots had difficulty getting objects from them, since most couldn't see that high and reach with their arms at the same time. He was impressed, too, by their strength, since they could carry more items and much larger, heavier items than humans could.

Then, it was time for the Neanderthals' meal break. One of the floor supervisors rang the bell to let them know it was time to get their bowls of meat and bread from the mechanical cart that rolled up and down the aisle. It stopped when one or more Neanderthals came close to it to get their lunch or dinner.

Dan watched them eat standing in small groups, and when another bell rang after 15 minutes, they dutifully returned to finding packages and putting them on the conveyor belt.

"Good," he thought to himself, "everything's running so perfectly.

Then, for a moment, Dan worried: "What could possibly go wrong?" But he quickly brushed the thought away, as he turned the operations over to Jack Burns, the night shift manager, and stopped by John's office behind the shipping facility.

"I'm off now. Everything's fine, so don't work too hard," Dan said.

John looked up from the budget and cash projections he was reviewing.

"Oh, don't worry about that," he called back playfully. "I never do."

Then, as he looked at the projections, he imagined teams of Neanderthals replicating themselves as they got hired doing all kinds of tasks he imagined they could do. He could picture them working on farms instead of humans and mechanical pickers. They could work on road construction crews all over the U.S. and in Alaska and Canada, and better withstand the cold than humans. They might work with loggers clearing the forests in designated areas to reduce fire danger and provide more land for farming and mining. Maybe they could even join teams of wrestlers and boxers to add a new dimension to the sport.

Yes, there were so many things that he imagined the Neanderthals could do if there were enough of them. "But give it time," he thought. "Just give us some more time, and our company can produce more and more Neanderthals."

He imagined the company just needed seven years for each new generation, and so far his company was the only one producing Neanderthal workers. "If only we can keep it that way," he thought, as he looked at more budget projections, and saw the millions upon millions of dollars adding up.

CHAPTER 14: RECRUITING THE FORCE

A few days later, when the shipping operations were humming along as usual, John was going over records in his office when Jane Winston, the receptionist at the front desk, called him on the intercom.

"There are some men here who want to speak to you."

John glanced at his calendar.

"I wasn't expecting anyone."

"They said it's important."

John frowned, annoyed.

"Well, tell them they have to set up an appointment. Everyone thinks whatever they want to discuss is important. I need to know what they want to talk about so I can prepare."

Jane got ready to shoo the men away and began telling them: "The CEO is busy now. But he'd like me to find out more about what you want so I can set up a meeting."

"Make it now," one of the men said, and he flashed a badge.

Jane called John back.

"They're from the local police force. They're detectives," she said.

John held the intercom silently for a few moments, stunned and suddenly scared.

"Did they say why they're here?" he said.

"No. Just that they want to talk to you now."

John glanced nervously at the photo of the Neanderthals working in the warehouse.

"God, what do they want?" he worried, as he imagined the worst. Maybe the detectives had somehow heard about the Neanderthal workers and now had all kinds of charges in mind - - hiring undocumented workers, having them work in unsafe conditions, or not paying wages, so maybe this could be considered human slavery. But then he could explain how he had treated them very well and humanely by providing meal breaks, education, and plenty of time between shifts for relaxation and recreation. So what could the problem be?

Then, he heard Jane's voice again saying "Sir?" and he jerked out of his reverie.

"Okay. Go ahead. Send them up," he said.

He adjusted his tie and sat up straight to look as professional and businesslike as possible.

Then, a knock on the door.

"Come in," he said.

Three men in matching blue suit jackets and ties strode in.

"I'm Lieutenant Jack Davis with the investigative detective unit of the Franklin P.D.," he said. "And this is Sergeant Don Burrows and Sergeant Will Garrett."

The detectives sat down in three chairs across from John.

"We heard about your Neanderthals," Lt. Davis said, "and we wanted to talk to you about that."

John felt beads of sweat form on his forehead, and he hoped the detectives didn't notice how scared he was.

"Uhhh, how did you hear about them?" John asked.

"We can't tell you," Lt. Davis said. "We just learned they were working for you in your shipping department."

John nodded. "Yes, that's true."

He flashed back to his meeting a few days before with Stan and his associates signing a million dollar contract. Was that how the detectives knew? Was Stan a spy for them? If so, was the million dollar contract just a ploy to get information and get him convicted of some crime? Then, how did Stan find out about the Neanderthals, since he was so careful to work on referrals only. Who else might have shared this information?

"If you can tell us more about what they are doing for you, that would be helpful," Lt. Davis said.

At once, John snapped back to their conversation.

"What do you want to know? What's wrong? Maybe I should bring in my lawyer before I talk to you? Am I...under arrest?"

Lt. Davis and his two associates laughed.

"Oh, no," Lt. Davis said. "We're not here to charge you with anything. We thought maybe you could help us, and maybe we could hire some Neanderthals, too."

"What?"

John sat back stunned, not sure what to say.

"That's right. We're working undercover on some cases, where we could use some help. So, of course, any work they do for us will be confidential. No one else will know. Not even the officers in other departments or the higher ups in the police force. We'll just call them confidential informants, if that's okay with you?"

"Okay with me? With me?" John thought. He could hardly believe what the officers were saying. He wasn't in trouble, and they were offering him a deal. He could barely think of what to say or do, so he just sat silently, thinking about how to respond.

"And we'll pay them, of course," Lt. Davis said. "Or pay you, and you can take care of their compensation."

"Yes, that'll be fine," John managed.

"Okay, then, we agree," Lt. Davis said. "We'll work out the details and send you a contract. We'd like to start with six Neanderthals. We thought they might make a good squad."

"Of course," John agreed.

"And please, pick out your best men for the job. What we need are guys that are strong, aggressive, have really good vision, and can work well together as a group, like Neanderthals do when out on a hunt. At least that's what we read about them."

John nodded, amazed as he listened.

"Because that's what we want them for. We're on a hunt for one really bad criminal who escaped from prison, and we've got him located in the desert near some mountains and caves. But our guys don't have the skills or smarts to go there. So when we heard about the Neanderthals, we thought that's it. A perfect fit. They can go there to find him, and it's something we can't do."

Lt. Davis laughed. "And of course we can't send in any robots to do this. We need some actual humans to go there, or more precisely some humans with the kinds of qualities the Neanderthals are known for. So what do you say? Can we do this together?"

"Yes, yes," said John, trying to contain his mounting excitement so he wouldn't seem too eager, as he negotiated the terms of the deal. "I'd like to do that, and I think we can all make a good team."

"Very good," said Lt. Davis. "And remember, this assignment has to be hush hush. No one can know. At least for now, while the Neanderthals do their first assignment. Otherwise, the top brass and others in the department could think we're crazy and out of line. But the guys in our undercover unit talked about it, and we feel sure it'll work."

Lt. Davis and his associates got up. He reached across the table and shook hands with John.

"Okay, then. We'll talk more in the next few days and I'll bring over the contract. We'll have lots to discuss about our plans for this first operation."

He paused at the door.

"Oh, and lets call this Neanderthal team something. How about the New Neanderthals Force? It is new, though a little ironic isn't it, since these guys go back many thousands of years.

He chuckled as he and his associates walked through the door and John watched them go.

The New Neanderthal Force, he thought to himself. Nice, straightforward, and simple. He thought the Neanderthal team he selected would like it, too.

CHAPTER 15: FINDING THE FIRST SIX

A few days after signing the contract, Lt. Davis and Sergeants Burrows and Garrett met with John and Dan to tour the shipping facility, so they could select the six Neanderthals for the force. As they walked around, the Neanderthal workers rushed around as usual selecting items, putting them in packages and on the conveyer belt.

"We want the best individuals from your facility for this assignment," Lt. Davis explained. "You know, the best of your best."

"Understood," John said.

He pointed out different Neanderthals as they walked around, referring to them by the numbers on the back of their loose fitting shirts.

"That's how we keep track of them," Dan said. "That way we can know who's where and what they are doing."

"The numbers are fine," Lt. Davis replied. "But once we select them, we'll give them names. We want them to feel a special pride at being chosen for this elite unit."

"And that'll breed loyalty, too," Sgt. Burrows added. "To each other and the whole unit."

"Well, we used numbers because there are so many of them," John replied a little defensively. "But we treat them really well. With plenty of good food, and time for breaks, sleep, and recreation."

"Of course," Lt. Davis said, reassuringly. "We'll be using them for special assignments. So we want to do that little bit extra, so they'll be good loyal soldiers. We want to build esprit de corps."

They continued walking, and from time to time, John pointed out one of the stand-out Neanderthals.

"That's 2604," he said, as they stopped by a Neanderthal putting large TVs in boxes. "He's really strong. So we use him for especially big packages."

"Good," said Lt. Davis. "We'll add him to the group. And we'll give him a name. What about Adam, since he's the first?"

"Then, Adam it is," said John, making a note that 2604 would now be called Adam.

John motioned for Adam to finish packing up a TV and come with them.

"You'll be joining Lt. Davis for a special job," John said.

"Okay, yes, sir," Adam said, stepping behind Lt. Davis.

The group walked on past a few rows of shelves to the conveyer belt. They stopped behind a Neanderthal with the number 3048 on his shirt.

"This is 3048," John said. "He's been especially alert when there have been problems with the conveyers slowing down or packages bunching up. Then, he signals the human supervisor to speed up the belt or stop it."

"Sounds like just what we need," said Lt. Davis. "Invite him to join the group. And let's call him Brad, since he's the second to join us. If we use the ABCs, it'll be easier to remember everyone's name."

"So noted," said John, making the notation on his list of Neanderthal numbers and corresponding names.

Brad left his station by the conveyer belt and stepped into the group beside Adam.

Then, John continued leading the group around the shipping facility, pointing out different Neanderthals he thought did an especially good job at something.

At the end of the tour, six Neanderthals were lined up in two rows behind Lt. Davis and Sergeants Burrows and Garrett -- Adam, Brad, Charlie, Derrick, Eddy, and Fred.

John led everyone into his office behind the shipping facility.

"Have a seat everyone," he said.

He motioned for everyone to sit down around the conference table.

The Neanderthals looked around, gazing at the walls, tables, and everyone at the table with amazement, since they had never seen such a room before.

John smiled broadly at each of the Neanderthals to show they were welcome and this was a supportive, friendly meeting. He spoke slowly, with the simple words the Neanderthals had learned in their training when they were growing up and when they began working in the facility.

"You'll be joining a new special group. You'll go with Lt. Davis. He'll take care of you and train you for your new job."

He paused, to check that the Neanderthals were following his explanation, then continued.

"You will have new names, too. They will be names like humans have. No more numbers."

The Neanderthals grinned as he spoke.

"Good, they seem to see this is an honor," John thought.

He pointed to each Neanderthal in turn.

"You're Adam...You're Brad...You're Charlie...You're Derrick...You're Eddy...You're Fred."

The Neanderthals nodded as John named them, and then he continued.

"Now you'll be going with Lt. Davis. He will have special work for you. You'll like it. You will learn new skills. You will work together as a group. You will live in a new place just for you. And it will be fun."

Again, John paused, making sure the Neanderthals understood and would go along with whatever Lt. Davis planned for them.

For a few moments, the Neanderthals signaled to each other with hand signs and smiles.

Then, Adam, spoke. "Yes. We know. It'll be good. We like to learn."

John, Dan, Lt. Davis and the sergeants leaned back, relieved that the changeover seemed to go smoothly, much better than they had thought. They were pleased that the Neanderthals understood, liked what they were doing, and could even speak.

"Very good," said John. "Now follow Lt. Davis and he'll take you to your new home and job."

Lt. Davis and the sergeants stood up, and Lt. Davis motioned for the Neanderthals to follow him. Pushing their chairs behind them, the Neanderthals formed a line as they followed Lt. Davis and the sergeants out the door. Adam walked in front, followed by Brad, then Charlie, and lastly by Derrick, Eddy, and Fred.

John marveled at how they followed the detectives out in a line. It was as if each Neanderthal knew his place and was ready to follow the leader, based on the order in which they had been chosen.

"I'll keep you posted on how everything is going," Lt. Davis called back.

"Thanks," John said and watched a little wistfully as the group left. He had grown fond of the Neanderthals and would miss the ones he sent away.

But then he looked down at the signed contract on the table with the first $10,000 payment for the six workers, and he felt better already.

"It'll be fine," he thought to himself. "It's gonna be fine."

CHAPTER 16: TRAINING DAYS

Once in front of the shipping facility, the Neanderthals got into the cars with the detectives, two in each of their cars. Lt. Davis led the convoy to the small house in the country, where they would live and train over the next few weeks. Once they were ready, they would get their first assignment.

The house was located in a clearing in the woods at the end of a windy narrow road that snaked off from the main highway. Lt Davis thought the location ideal, because he wanted someplace very private, so he could keep the program secret from the top brass and others in the department. And he certainly didn't want the media to know, since the Neanderthal project was a pilot program. He wanted to be sure it would work, before unveiling it to higher ups or the world.

As Lt. Davis drove, he shifted his glance back and forth from the road to watching Adam and Brad in the back seat. They looked around eagerly, fascinated by all the cars around them as they sped along the freeway. When Lt. Davis turned onto the side road, they became even more excited as they saw the trees hugging the side of the road.

Excitedly, they spun around, looking at the side windows and then out back, pointing their fingers and speaking quickly to each other in short phrases.

"Look, trees."

"Green plants."

"Red flowers."

"And see the big rocks."

"So many trees."

Lt. Davis was glad to hear them talking. That would make teaching them even easier if they already understood basic words and short sentence. Then, he could teach them more.

Finally, the house with dark brown wooden planks appeared in the distance.

"We're almost there," he told Adam and Brad.

Once they arrived, the other two cars with the other four Neanderthals pulled in behind them.   Lt. Davis waved for the others to follow him to the house.

Inside, he led the Neanderthals to their three bedrooms, each about 12x15 feet with two bunk beds, The Neanderthals quickly divided up, two to a room, as if they already knew the drill.   Adam and Brad took the first bedroom, Charlie and Derrick took the second, Eddy and Fred took the third, and the first man in each group took the bottom bunk.

"Amazing," said Lt. Davis to Sergeants Burrows and Garrett, as the Neanderthals settled in. "They're already so disciplined, like a military unit. Just think if we took six random guys off a factory floor and brought them here. It would be chaos as they fought each other for the best room and lower bunk."

"Yeah, I noticed that," said Sgt. Burrows. "Having this military spirit will certainly help when we train them."

"And when we assign them to help with an investigation, such as finding and catching a criminal," Sgt. Garrett added.

"Exactly," said Lt. Davis. "Maybe they can help us with the things we can't do ourselves."

"Let's hope so," Sgt. Burrows agreed. "Otherwise..."

Lt. Davis interrupted him. "Don't worry. Whatever the outcome, we'll find a way to bury whatever we spend in the budget. It'll be our secret for now. Then if the training works out, we'll introduce them to the rest of the detective squad."

* * * * * *

The following day, the training began, led by Lt. Davis and the two sergeants. The plan was to teach the Neanderthals basic outdoor and indoor skills for following suspects, discovering where they were hiding, flushing them out, and ultimately trapping them. Then, the cops could arrest them and bring them in.

As the Neanderthals gathered in the living room, as a fire burned in the fireplace, Lt. Davis explained the basics.

"We'll be teaching you some new skills. We'll start with what you already know how to do. We'll learn what you are good at. Then, we'll help you get even better. That way you can help us. Sound good?"

The Neanderthals nodded. "Yes, sir," they said, almost in unison.

"Then let us begin."

Soon after that, Lt. Davis and the sergeants began training them. They divided the Neanderthals into two groups and showed them how to run around the woods and find where members of the other group were hiding. They demonstrated how to sneak up on others, tag them, and tie ropes around them to capture them, much like they might sneak up on a deer or panther in the wild. The detectives also gave them spears modeled after the spears Neanderthals once used and invited them to throw them at targets. They showed them new ways to communicate with each other by using whistles that sounded like bird calls.

They then asked the Neanderthals what they might do if they were chasing someone who didn't want to be caught.

"We can trap him," said Adam.

He and Brad then demonstrated how Adam might come from one direction, Brad from another. If they needed more help, Charlie and Derrick might appear from still another direction, while Eddy and Fred might wait in hiding. This way, as a team, they could capture the person when he tried to run away.

Day after day, the Neanderthals kept practicing different moves, and Lt. Davis noticed how the Neanderthals ran faster and faster and grew stronger and stronger as they worked out. They especially liked to charge their opponent with simple natural weapons, such as sticks, rocks, and even dirt which they could pick up and throw. But they could use modern weapons, too, such as when Lt. Davis handed them a baton, throwing stick, boomerang, or stick with a ball and chain, and they charged with it or threw it. The more they practiced, the better they became at hitting their targets or capturing the straw dummies that Lt. Davis and the sergeants used to simulate the criminals they hunted.

Finally, after several weeks of practicing different techniques, Lt. Davis decided they were ready.

"Now let's see if they can help us for real," he told Sergeants Burrows and Garrett.

"What do you mean?" Sgt. Burrows asked.

"Well, I was thinking about a prison escapee who is still hiding out in the dessert or the mountains. The police have given up on him. But maybe the Neanderthals can track him down and capture him.   We sure haven't able to do that ourselves. We can't even find him."

So that's how it started -- putting the Neanderthals to work on an actual case.

When Lt. Davis told the Neanderthals their plans, they were excited.

"Sounds very good," said Adam.

"I like it," said Brad.

"And it'll be very cool, as you say," said Charlie.

Lt. Davis thought the Neanderthals were more than ready. They had even been picking up on their own speech patterns. Now what could they do in the field? Lt. Davis and Sergeants Burrows and Garrett were eager to find out.

CHAPTER 17: THE FIRST MISSION

Early the next morning, Lt. Davis, flanked by Sgt. Burrows and Sgt. Garrett, met in the Neanderthals' cabin. The Neanderthals, wearing light blue shirts and jeans, stood in the living room in a semi-circle in front of him, like a military unit awaiting their orders.

"Okay. We have a project for you," Lt. Davis said. 'It will show what you can do. It's for real this time."

The Neanderthals listened quietly, like soldiers awaiting more details.

"Do you understand?"

The Neanderthals nodded in unison.

Lt. Davis continued. "Okay. We have to find this guy. He killed people and escaped from prison."

Lt. Davis held up a picture of the prisoner and passed it to Adam, who looked at it, passed it to Brad, who similarly looked at it and passed it on. After Fred, the last in line, looked at it, he brought it back to Lt. Davis.

"Okay. That's who you will look for," Lt. Davis said. "You'll have these weapons if you need them. And some water, too."

Sgt. Burrows and Sgt. Garrett stepped forward with six backpacks. Sgt. Burrows opened one of them and placed the contents on the floor beside it -- a baton, a throwing stick, a hunting boomerang, a stick with a ball and chain, and some rocks -- the same weapons they had been practicing with. Then, Sgt. Garrett stepped forward with six spears and gave one to each Neanderthal.

"In case you want to use this," Lt. Davis said. "Just think of this search like hunting for game."

The Neanderthals smiled happily as Lt. Davis continued. "You just have to find him for us. Then, you have to surround him. You want to keep him where he is."

"That's so he can't get away," Sgt. Burrows added.

"Trap him?" Adam asked.

"That's right," Lt. Davis said. "Trap him and hold him there."

"Then, we'll come and get him," Sgt. Garrett added.

"Yes, do that," said Lt. Davis. "Or maybe bring him to us. Either way, we'll take it from there."

Adam glanced around at the other Neanderthals, who each nodded in turn.

"Okay. We do it. We help you. We want to help," Adam said.

With that, the meeting was over.

Lt. Davis and Sergeants Burrows and Garrett led the Neanderthals to their cars parked on the road to the cabin. The Neanderthals, carrying their spears and backpacks, got in, just as they had before -- Adam and Brad in the first car with Lt. Davis, Charlie and Derrick in the next car with Sgt. Burrows, and finally Eddy and Fred in the last car with Sgt. Garrett.

Then, the cars sped off, heading toward the road through the desert where the prison escapee was last seen.

* * * * * *

A few hours later, the cars were driving on a narrow dirt road that ran alongside a wide expanse of desert. In the distance, the spikes of rocky hills and mountains shot up, looking like a barren moonscape. An old Ford pickup truck was parked in the dirt by the roadside, and a few footsteps led away from it in the mud. A few feet out, the sands of the desert covered up any prints.

Lt. Davis stopped behind the truck and got out of his car, followed by the sergeants and Neanderthals. As the Neanderthals assembled in a row in front of him, Sgt. Burrows and Sgt. Garrett joined him, one standing on either side.

114

"This is where we need you to find the prisoner," he said to the Neanderthals.

He turned to Sgt. Burrows and Sgt. Garrett and pointed to the truck. "This is where the prisoner abandoned his stolen truck, since he ran out of gas. So he's probably somewhere out there, since no one picked him up. About a week ago, the department got a call about this abandoned stolen truck."

Lt. Davis turned back to the Neanderthals. He pointed to the tracks in the mud leading to the desert.

"He's out there somewhere. His tracks end here."

The Neanderthals gathered around him to look at the tracks.

"So you go out there," Lt. Davis continued. "See if you can find him."

"We try," Adam said.

Lt. Davis reached in his pocket and pulled out a cell phone. He reached out to hand it to Adam, telling him.

"You can reach us on this phone. Call us if you need help. Or call if you find him. I'll show you how it works."

But Adam pushed his hand away.

"No. We do it our way. We find him. We capture him for you."

Lt. Davis pulled back his hand with the phone.

"Okay. Do it your way. And come back if you don't find him, too."

Adam glanced around, as the other Neanderthals nodded their agreement.

"Okay. We will," Adam said.

"And good luck to all of you," Lt. Davis said.

As the Neanderthals set off, Lt. Davis the sergeants waved, and the Neanderthals waved back.

As he watched them walk away on the steaming hot sands, Lt. Davis worried. What if they got lost and didn't come back? What if they found the criminal and he shot one or more of them dead? What if they succumbed to the desert heat? What if?

He turned to Sgt. Burrows and Sgt. Garrett.

"I was just thinking whether we should be doing this? After all, these guys will be exposed in the desert to all the elements. And Adam wouldn't even take my cell phone in case they need any help."

"Look, don't worry. These guys are pretty strong and resourceful," Sgt. Burrows said.

"And at least this project is still secret. So no one else but us knows about it, if things go south," said Sgt. Garrett.

"That's what worries me, too," Lt. Davis said. "No one else knows about this. So we can't call on anyone in the department for help. And the prison has already given up on finding their escaped prisoner in the desert. It's too expensive to search, and if he doesn't turn up anywhere else, they think he's dead."

"So we just have to wait," said Sgt. Burrows.

"Yeah, we just wait," Lt. Davis agreed.

CHAPTER 18: KEEP ON TRACKING

Adam and the other Neanderthals waved back as they walked away. Then, they looked around at the sands that stretched out like a bumpy carpet and at the rock strewn hills and mountains in the distance. A few lumpy white clouds fluttered by in the light blue sky.

Suddenly, it felt very freeing to be outside that musty cabin or in the woods that surrounded the cabin like a wall of trees. It had felt freeing to run around in the woods playing hide and seek and "I found you" games. But the time outside soon ended, and they were back in the cabin that felt like a prison with its small rooms and stacked up bunk beds.

Now here they were ready to do what they loved doing best -- go hunting for something, anything. And if they could help their masters, Lt. Davis and the two sergeants, that was even better.

"Look!" Adam called out and pointed to the spot where the track seemed to end where the mud turned to sand.

The other Neanderthals gathered around him to look closely at the disappearing footprints.

"We have to find where they go," Adam said. "Man out there somewhere."

Adam pointed to the wide expense of desert and rocks.

"So we look hard. We find."

Adam took a stick from his backpack. He pushed some of the sand away from where the footprints disappeared.

"See. Some footprints still there. We can follow."

Adam moved more sand aside, as the other Neanderthals followed behind him. With the sand removed, Adam saw the faint imprint of a trail the detectives hadn't seen.

The footprints went on for about a mile, a continuing trail left under the sand. Then, it stopped.

Adam and the other Neanderthals looked around. What happened? They looked around, and the sand sparkled in the sun like a large lake surrounded by rocky mountains on one side and a few trees by the road on the other.

"Let's rest and think what could happen," Adam said.

The others sat down around him. They dug into their backpacks, drank from their canteens, and ate some of the nuts and berries Lt. Davis and the sergeants had packed for them.

"Maybe wind. Maybe rain," Adam said finally. "So maybe we have to look further."

The other Neanderthals agreed, and soon they pushed the sand aside in ever widening circles. Meanwhile, the hot desert sun bore down on them. They found collapsible straw hats in their backpacks and put them on, though they still sweated in the fierce desert heat.

Finally, Brad pushed aside some sand and noticed some tracks.

"We found them!" he cried out, and everyone gathered around the soft heel impressions in the ground.

"Good, we dig through the sand here," Adam said.

So they continued pushing the sand aside in their new location. On and on they dug through the sand until the tracks led to the rocks and craggy hills surrounding the desert.

"We're here. He's somewhere here," Adam announced. "No more footprints in the rocks. But we still find him."

Three of the Neanderthals started to move ahead towards the rocks.

"No, wait!" Adam called out. "We must go slowly. We must plan. We have to see him first before he sees us."

So the Neanderthals gathered in a circle by the entrance to the rocks and hills, as the late afternoon sun sank lower in the sky and the shadows deepened. They welcomed the growing coolness and coming darkness.

"This will help us," Adam told everyone. "We just have to wait a little longer. We see if he's somewhere. Then, we find him, bring him in."

Meanwhile, Lt. Davis and the sergeants waited nervously by the truck, wondering what was happening.

"We'll be on assignment a little bit longer," Lt. Davis called in to headquarters. But he didn't tell the officer who answered what the assignment was.

CHAPTER 19: UNDER THE COVER OF DARKNESS

As the darkness settled in, Adam urged everyone to wait a little longer.

"We wait now till best," he said. "And we stay quiet. No one must hear us."

So they all sat quietly, resting on their haunches or sitting on the desert floor.

Soon the moon rose slowly in the eastern sky. It was only a three quarter moon, not as bright as a full moon, but its light cast an eerie glow across the rocks. Though Lt. Davis had put flashlights in their packs, the Neanderthals didn't want to use them, not wanting to show anyone where they were. Instead, they could travel silently in the faint light of the moon.

When the moon was about halfway up in the sky, Adam signaled to the others.

"Okay. Everyone ready. We can go."

"But how find him?" Brad asked.

"We just look, watch. Look for animals moving. Maybe they call out to others. Maybe birds circle if he's hurt, bleeding. So we move slowly. Watch."

Waving for the others to follow, Adam moved through the first circle of rocks on the ground towards the rocky hills and outcroppings.

Then he stopped, and so did the others. Now they listened and looked for any signs of where the prisoner might be hiding, if he was still in the rocky hills somewhere.

Suddenly, a fox appeared, its eyes glistening yellow in the moonlight. It stared at the Neanderthals, and they stared back. Unnerved, the fox loped away.

Then came a coyote and wolf. They each stopped about 25 feet away behind a wall of boulders and bushes, watching the Neanderthals with fiery eyes.

"They are just checking us out," Adam told the others. "We are in their land. So they want to see what we are doing."

"But we mean no harm," said Charlie.

"No," said Adam. "So they will soon go away."

After a few minutes the coyote and wolf became tired of waiting and trotted off.

Meanwhile, Adam and the Neanderthals waited and listened.

Hearing nothing but the wind, rustling bushes, and calls of birds, they moved a little closer. They settled in between some large rocks that were like a doorway to the hills beyond.

"Are we in the right place to look?" Eddy wanted to know.

Adam reassured him. "Yes. The footprints ended near here. So this is where he came to the rocks."

The Neanderthals settled back down again. It was a little like waiting by one of many entrances to a building, knowing this is where a person entered and then waited in the vast lobby, while deciding where to go next.

As the minutes ticked by, the Neanderthals heard the hooting of owls, the chatter of birds in the trees, the flapping wings of flying birds, and the chirp of crickets. Sometimes they heard one animal call to another. But nothing suggested that the escapee was even there.

Meanwhile, with the sun gone, the desert air was getting colder and colder, while the wind was blowing more strongly. The Neanderthals shivered a little and pulled their rabbit fur jackets from their backpacks. They put them on, and moved closer to each other to keep warm.

"Just keep waiting," Adam reassured them, knowing they were getting tired, impatient, and bored just waiting in silence.

Then, he noticed a few wisps of smoke rise high in the sky. They glowed slightly from the light of the moon.

"That's it!" he announced. "Maybe smoke from his campfire. He wants to get warm, too."

Adam got up and motioned for the others to follow him. Slowly, the Neanderthals moved on, very quietly as they walked with bare feet, toughened by years of growing up without wearing shoes. They walked between the rocks or scrambled over them.

Meanwhile, the wisps of smoke grew fatter and longer, as they got closer, perhaps 50 yards away. Now Adam and the other Neanderthals could smell the musky scene of burning wood.

"We're getting close," Adam said.

But as they came within 25 yards and Adam was certain the prisoner was there, he told the others to spread out.

"We want to surround him," he whispered.

Then, with a few hand signals, he told Brad to go behind him. He motioned for Charlie and Derrick to go to the right, and Eddy and Frank to go to the left.

"You go there, and I'll keep moving forward," he said quietly.

Then, keeping the rising smoke in view, the Neanderthals spread out, taking positions about 20 yards from the smoke and slowly, quietly, closing in.

Since they could no longer speak, the Neanderthals used bird calls to signal to each other -- one hoot to indicate they were in position, two hoots to indicate they were moving closer, three hoots to indicate they were even closer. They moved much like the Neanderthals might close in to trap a bison or mammoth, but now they were surrounding a prisoner, and they carried some ropes in their backpacks if needed to tie him up to bring him in. They knew not to charge in for the kill and spear the prisoner to death.

After about 20 minutes, Adam felt they were close enough to rush in and spring their trap. He could even hear the prisoner moving logs in the fire.

So he gave the signal -- four long hoots. At once, the Neanderthals all ran silently toward the prisoner, like a pack of stealthy running wolves.

Closer and closer they all came -- 15 yards, 10 yards, 5 yards.

Now they saw the burning fire and the man huddled in blankets by the fire. It seemed like it would be an easy attack. In moments the six of them could surround him, grab him, and throw their ropes around him. Then, they could force him to walk with them down the mountain and back to the desert where Lt. Davis and the sergeants would be waiting.

But suddenly, crack! Derrick stepped on a branch, which snapped with a crackle.

At once the prisoner looked up in the direction of the sound and pulled out his gun. Then, he began shooting.

Derrick heard the loud pop of the gun and fell to the ground, as the bullet tore into the tree behind him. Seconds later, another gunshot and another followed, plowing into a nearby bush and then smashing against the rock next to him.

Derrick had never heard gunshots before, and the Neanderthals had never gotten any training on what to do if someone shot at them. So he cowered motionless on the ground, afraid to move, not sure what to do next. He just knew that whatever was shooting at him was very powerful and something he couldn't do anything about. He just knew, as he saw the nearby trees and bushes quiver with each loud whizzing sound, that he had to avoid whatever it was. So he held on tight to the earth beneath him. He hoped that the shooting would stop and he would still be alive when the shooting was over.

CHAPTER 20: FIGHTING ON

After several minutes, the shots aimed at Derrick stopped, though he lay still for several more minutes, afraid to stand up and face more shooting.

Meanwhile, Adam hooted to Brad, Charlies, Eddy, and Fred to see if they were all right. Yes, they hooted back, we're fine, and he hooted back to tell them to wait.

Then, Adam had an idea. He picked up a stone and threw it, so it crashed to earth about 10 feet away. At once a series of shots rang out, aimed at wherever the rock had fallen. When the shooting stopped, Adam stealthily moved closer and threw another rock. Again, there were more shots at the rock target, followed by another few minutes of silence, and he moved closer yet.

After he threw the third rock, Adam crept over to where Eddie and Fred stood behind bushes to his left. He saw them waiting in the moonlight, and as soon as he came close, he whispered: "Throw rocks. Aim them far away."

Eddie and Fred quickly threw the rocks about 10 feet in either direction. When more shots rang out hitting several trees and rocks, Adam smiled and whispered. "Good. We know where he is. Throw more rocks and tell Brad."

As Eddie threw rocks, Fred slowly and stealthily walked to where Brad was hunkered down behind some bushes. At the same time, Adam snuck back to where he had been.

When Charles and Derrick realized what the others were doing, they began to throw rocks, too, that landed far to their left or right. At the same time, they all crept closer and closer to the prisoner by the fire. 20 feet, 15 feet, 12 feet.

Soon they could see the prisoner by the campfire holding his gun and aiming wildly, scared that an army of soldiers were coming toward him and getting closer and closer, as the pounding of what sounded like boots stomping became louder and louder.

Only 10 feet away, and the Neanderthals could see the sweat pouring down the prisoner's forehead. 8 feet away, and the pounding for the prisoner was even louder. Louder! Louder!

Finally, the prisoner stood up and threw down his gun.

"Don't shoot. Don't shoot. I'll surrender. I'll go with you," he yelled. "I don't want to die."

He stood shaking, a lone figure by fire, the flames flickering across his belly, while the moonlight shone on him like he was lit by a spotlight on stage.

At this, Adam gave another hoot. In moments, all of the Neanderthals surrounded the prisoner. They grabbed ropes from their backpacks, draped them around him, and pulled them tight, while the prisoner shook and shivered all over.

"You come with us," Adam said.

"Yes. Yes," said the prisoner, who couldn't see the Neanderthals as well as they could see him. So he thought they were regular cops or prison guards who had caught him.

"Wherever you want," he added. "I'm tired of running. I'm cold. I'm tired. I'm ready to go back."

Adam smiled broadly. "Okay. We take you back now."

Then, with Adam leading the way, Brad and Charlie on either side, and Derrick, Eddy, and Fred bringing up the rear, the Neanderthals led the prisoner back down the rocky mountain and across the desert.

In the distance, they saw Lt. Davis and the sergeants waiting for them.

Adam waved and hooted. "We back. We back."

Lt. Davis could barely believe it. The Neanderthals and the prisoner were returning so quickly and so peaceably.

He turned to Sgt. Burrows and Sgt. Garrett.

"Can you believe it? They did it. They really did. Dozens of police officers and guards couldn't find the prisoner, but they did."

"Yeah," said Sgt. Burrows. "And if they did that, just think what else they might do."

"I know," said Lt. Davis. "Let's think about that. Let's think about our other unsolved cases and what else we can do."

PART III: THE NEW NEANDERTHALS GANG

CHAPTER 21: CREATING THE GANG

When Ray Hammond read about the success of the New World Neanderthal's project, he was pissed. He had a thriving team of thieves, burglars, robbers, and occasional hit men who had been working well. His business of selling counterfeit goods from China and black market weed was thriving, since they were much cheaper than the real or legal goods. Plus, he knew how to outwit most of the cops in the San Francisco Bay Area and L.A., and he had lawyers who could swoop in when one of his guys got arrested and get him released on bail and at least get no time or a few months. Then, his team of Neanderthals would soon be back in action.

But now this. Ray angrily threw down the newspaper and stared out of the window of his home in an exclusive suburban community. He found it a welcome retreat from working at his warehouse office in the city.

What could he do about the situation, he wondered? The last thing he needed was national attention focused on how the New World Neanderthals were tracking down hard to find criminals for the police. Worse, one of his gang members, Dan Healy, had been busted when he fled into the hills and tried to bury a half a million in jewelry. The damned force had been able to track him there by withstanding both the searing desert heat and the freezing cold nights in the hills. Then, they had even found where Dan hid the jewelry after the cops arrived and took him in. So now both the jewelry and the money from its sale were gone, and Dan would spend a long time in jail.

Ray picked up his cell phone and called his associate, Jeff Travers, who worked as his right hand man in handling operations.

"Jeff," he said. "What are we going to do? It's a big story now about how the cops used a team of Neanderthals to track down our thieves. And the next thing you know, the cops can have their Neanderthals taking down our guys and messing up our operations."

"I know," Jeff replied. "It's really bad, because people think of these guys as heroes. So each time the Neanderthals help the cops bust a criminal or stop a crime that could be money out of our pockets. And when they get press, they have the help of citizens calling in leads. Then, because of all the press, the prosecutors are tougher than usual and the deals are worse. Or there are no deals at all."

"Yeah, it's a tragedy," Ray said. "So what can we do?"

Jeff thought for a minute, then replied. "Why not fight fire with fire? I mean, why not create our own team of Neanderthals who we train to become criminals. They can then disrupt the missions of the New World Neanderthals team. In other words, they can help some criminals escape or the cops from finding and capturing criminals. Or they can draw the cops away, while our own guys get in and out of houses, deliver the goods, or otherwise steal and sell what they steal."

"Sounds good," said Ray. "And maybe we can even get the Neanderthals to do simple hits, say by throwing rocks or pushing someone off a cliff."

Ray reflected quietly on the possibilities, then continued, "So how do we do it? How do you suggest we find and train these Neanderthals?"

"Well, we could go to that guy with the robot factory who's got a workforce of robots. He provided the Neanderthals to the cops who trained them. At least that's what I read," Jeff said.

"Hmmm," said Ray. "Tell me more. Since you're the operations guy here, how would this all work?"

"Simple. We get some Neanderthals who are already raised by the robot guy. They could be 15, 16, 17 years old. So they already know how to do regular work, like making stuff in the factory or shipping things. Then, we just buy them. The company owner doesn't have to know what we want the

Neanderthals for. After that, we take a few months to train them. And voila, we've got our own gang of Neanderthals, and we tell them to do what we want."

"Brilliant idea, Jeff," Ray said. "I'll get on it right away. So soon we can have our own crime gang to commit crimes for us and take on the Neanderthal Force, too."

CHAPTER 22: PREPARING FOR THE FIRST JOB

A week later, Ray had a team of six handpicked Neanderthals who had worked in the shipping facility. He thought that was a good number to start with since that's how many Neanderthals were working with the cops. Then, if the team worked out, he knew where he could quickly get more.

Then, with Jeff's help, he put together a training program with several associates who had special skills they could teach. The idea was to prepare the new Neanderthal gang members with some practice in the things they were supposed to be good at, such as setting up ambushes, aiming rocks, and attacking with spears, with new ways of applying these skills.

For example, Jerry Prince, AKA the Breaker, arrived to teach them about breaking, entering, and getting away quickly. Terry Wise, known as the Wise One, came to teach them about trapping victims in alleys and basements. Don Barry, called the Climber, was brought in to show how to climb and jump over walls. And Chip Gratton, known as Knuckles, because he knew how to break them, was invited to demonstrate how to jump a victim, push him down to the ground, and hold them there, while threatening to break his fingers or beat him up if he tried to resist.

To begin the training, Ray sent an assistant, Andy Flowers, to the cabin with bunk beds where the Neanderthals were staying. Andy lined them up in front of their bunks like a drill sergeant.

"Time for your training," Andy told them. "I'll be one of your trainers, and my name's Andy."

The Neanderthals followed him out and along the path to the main hall, where they formed into a line in front of him and Ray.

Andy began by asking them to run around the room and do push-ups and knee-bends. He demonstrated what to do before each activity. Then, Andy watched closely to see who seemed to be the fastest and strongest.

After the Neanderthals finished and lined up in front of the hall, Ray decided to give them names. He figured naming them after the most powerful and deadly bugs would be fitting and a good way to remember their names.

"Okay, I'm going to give you names," he announced to the group. "Then, pick your leader. Choose whoever you think is the strongest and most powerful."

Ray waited for minute, while the Neanderthals talked among themselves and looked back at him.

"Okay, now," he continued. "I'm gonna name you after some bugs I think are pretty cool. I know a lot of great guys with these names."

Ray looked around and picked out the Neanderthal who was a little taller than the others and had the biggest muscles.

"You're Scorpion," he said, "because they're one of the most deadly bugs there is. They have a thin tail with a stinger. And once they sting, that can leave someone feeling great pain. Their arms and legs can swell up and they can have trouble breathing. Their muscles can suddenly go haywire, too. So how do you like your name, Scorpion?"

"I do," Scorpion said.

Ray looked around the group, and picked out the Neanderthal standing to the right of Scorpion.

"Okay, you're Spider. They have a bite which is often deadly. And their bite can cause someone to having sore muscles, difficulty breathing, and a really bad stomach ache."

Again the Neanderthals whispered among themselves.

Then, Ray continued. "Okay, now that you have an idea of what these bugs can do, I'll quickly give you your names."

In turn, Ray pointed to the other four Neanderthals. He called the next one Wasp, then Yellow Jacket, then Hornet, and finally Tarantula.

"Now I hope you'll live up to your names. Because with Andy's help, I'm gonna train you to be really tough. That way you can help to protect us from the guys who are going after our guys. You can defend them and keep them from harm. You'll get to go after these guys who are after us. And we'll show you ways to get money for us, too."

Ray paused for a moment, while the Neanderthals turned to one another and quietly talked about his latest pronouncement. Then, they turned back towards him, waiting for his next instructions.

"All right, we'll begin," he said.

After that, Ray's associate Jeff joined him and Andy, and the three of them put the Neanderthals through their training that day and over the next few weeks. Each day, the training began with running and pushups, followed by a new technique. From time to time, Jerry Prince, the Breaker; Terry Wise, the Wise One; Don Barry, the Climber; and Chip Gratton, known as Knuckles; came to the training to demonstrate their special techniques.

One day, Ray and Jeff led the Neanderthal gang to an old abandoned factory. There, Jerry the Breaker showed them how to break through windows and doors. Then, he demonstrated how to stalk a victim without being seen.

"Now practice," Ray urged them, and for the next few days they practiced the two new techniques.

The next week, Don the Climber showed them how to climb over walls, scale fire escapes, and climb through rocky trails and cliffs.

After that, Chip, known as Knuckles, demonstrated various boxing and wrestling moves. He also showed them different ways to threaten a victim, and how to hit harder and harder if the victim kept resisting. Knuckles used cloth and plastic dummies to demonstrate, as Ray, Jeff, or Andy held them tight.

Meanwhile, as Ray and Jeff watched each day, they felt proud at how quickly the Neanderthals learned what to do.

"It seems natural for them," Ray commented after one session.

"That's right," Jeff agreed. "It must be in their genes. After all, they are built to be strong and aggressive."

"And now we're just directing their abilities to help us do what we want."

The men looked back at the training and smiled broadly.

"Just think, in a few weeks they'll go on their first real mission," Ray said.

"Yes," said Jeff. "And to think we trained them."

Then, Ray and Jeff returned to watching the Neanderthals train with Andy. Now Scorpion, Spider, and Tarantula were jumping high over hurdles, while Yellow Jacket, Hornet, and Wasp were beating the cloth dummies to shreds.

"I think they'll do very well," Ray commented. "And they seem to really enjoy it."

"That's right," Jeff said. "It's like they were born to do this. As they say, some are born to run. Well, these guys seem born to fight and kill."

"Exactly," Ray agreed. "Now let's see what they can do when we give them assignments to carry out real crimes or fight against the New World Neanderthals. If we had to bet, I'd say they win."

"Let's hope," said Jeff. "I'm ready to place my bet, too."

CHAPTER 23: GETTING READY TO FIGHT

The next day, Ray and Jeff call the Neanderthal gang in to give them their first assignment. They ran in like school kids going out to recess. Then, Ray and Jeff asked them to line up, with Scorpion and Spider in the center and Wasp and Yellow Jacket to their left, and Hornet and Tarantula to their right.

"Okay, very good," Ray said, as they got into formation. "You look like a real team. Now we'll tell you what we have planned."

Scorpion stepped forward, Spider just behind him.

"First we have a request," said Scorpion. "You have given us the names of insects. So we want to see those insects. We want to make them part of us."

Ray fell silent, dumbfounded. Jeff didn't know what to say either.

"It'll make us better fighters or do whatever you want us to do," said Spider.

"Yes," Scorpion said. "We will better understand these bugs and who we are. So we can call on their abilities to help us do what you want."

Ray nodded. "Okay. Let me see what I can do. I'll wait to give you your assignment. You can go back to your cabin, and I'll call you back when we're ready."

"Thank you," said Scorpion. "You be glad you wait."

After they left, Ray turned to Jeff.

"Geez. Where are we going to get some damned bugs to show them?."

"Maybe some photos would be fine," Jeff suggested. "Or maybe a video."

"No, no," Ray said. "We really have to get the real thing. But where?"

Ray and Jeff thought quietly for a few minutes.

Then, Jeff suggested, "What about online? I bet we could find some bug collectors."

So Ray tried a Google search for "Bug Collectors Near Me." At first, he only found companies that exterminated insects and advertised insect removal. But when he searched for "Bug Collectors," he discovered www.bugcollectors.com.

"How about contacting bug collectors?" he suggested to Jeff. "There are individuals all over the country who collect bugs. Some are even near here."

"But they put bugs in collections," Jeff said. "They dry them out and pin them in books and display cases."

"Yes, but before they do that, they catch them live. So we could recruit some of these bug collectors to find us the insects we want and pay them for the bugs they catch."

Jeff agreed "That's a good idea," and within two days, they had all the insects they needed.

The following day, they got the Neanderthals together again. This time, a table in front of Jeff held several glass display cases that looked like small fish tanks. But instead of fish swimming around, small groups of bugs crawled around: scorpions in one display case, spiders and tarantulas in another, and wasps, yellow jackets, and hornets in a third.

"Okay, I've got your bugs," Ray announced. "You can come look at them."

The Neanderthals got up excitedly and went over to the display of bugs with their name. They looked closely, much like bug collectors or scientists might carefully watch bugs and note their behavior.

Finally, Scorpion spoke. "This is good. I see how the scorpion moves. He crawls slowly. He approaches his prey. Then, he strikes with his tail and stings. I will think about that when I find the enemy. So I will move slowly, then strike with my hand or spear."

Next, Spider spoke about spiders. "He creates a web. He captures his prey in that. Then, he squashes or bites his prey and kills it. I can do that. Or maybe a group of us can create a web to trap the prey. Then, I go in and finish him off."

After that, Tarantula spoke. "I'm not like other spiders, because I live alone. And I don't make webs. I burrow into the ground. Then I crawl along quietly. I usually hunt at night. I sneak up on my prey and attack. I grab him with my legs and bite. So that's what I will learn to do. I'll look for the prey we are hunting at night, sneak up on him and grab him. I'll hold him tight."

As Scorpion, Spider, and Tarantula stepped away from their display cases, Ray and Jeff watched them in amazement. The three of them had carefully observed the behaviors of the bugs with their names and had learned so much by just watching them. No wonder they had wanted to see the bugs that were their namesakes, and certainly that would help them be better fighters in the field. And it could help to give them assignments where their special skills would pay off.

As Ray whispered quietly to Jeff, "You know, this discover your bug thing makes sense. I mean, Scorpion could really be good in attacking others, so he'd be the perfect hitman. Spider would work well with the team in tracking and surrounding a victim before coming in for the kill. And Tarantula would be especially good for night jobs. So if we think about the assignments, we could suggest different strategies to them."

"Good idea," said Jeff. "And maybe we could use some of these techniques with our regular guys. Let them learn how the bugs hunt and capture their prey. Why not? That could them some new ideas."

Then, it was time to learn what Yellow Jacket, Wasp, and Hornet had to say.

"We pretty much hang out together," said Yellow Jacket, "since we're just different types of wasps."

"Like a family," said Wasp.

"And mostly we fly around and sting," Hornet added. "So "we can move fast, attack quickly, and fly away."

"We're hard to catch, too," Wasp said.

"And we can work together to help each other," Yellow Jacket commented. "Or we can make someone coming after us confused, when we attack from all sides."

Ray and Jeff smiled. "That's very good. You all have a good idea of who you are and your abilities," Ray said. "So we think you're ready for first assignment."

"Yes, we're ready," said Scorpion, and the other Neanderthals nodded eagerly.

"Then, come back first thing in the morning, and we'll get started," Ray said.

As the Neanderthals filed out, Ray turned to Jeff.

"Do you know what you want them to do?" he asked.

"I do," said Jeff. "And I'll bring the plans with me tomorrow."

"Very good," said Ray. "And so it begins."

CHAPTER 24: FIRST ASSIGNMENT

The next morning, the Neanderthals lined up in their usual formation to hear their first assignment. They were dressed in jeans, shirts, and jackets with hoods so they would better blend into the neighborhood.

"Very good," said Ray, who stood before them, Jeff at his side.

He glanced down at the paper he was holding and continued.

"Okay, this is what you'll do. Jeff and I will drive you to the waterfront. You'll see docks and boats and a beach. Some of our rivals have gotten a shipment..."

Scorpion stepped forward and interrupted.

"Rivals? Shipment? What does that mean?"

"Oh, I forgot," said Ray. "Some of these words will be new to you. Rivals are like enemies. They are like fighters you are fighting.   A shipment is a delivery. It's like a package you receive."

"Thank you," said Scorpion stepping back into line.

Ray continued. "Anyway, the shipment will be on their boat that's docked there. Jeff will show you where that is."

Ray held up a photograph of the dock.

"We want you to find that package and bring it to us."

"But how we find it?" Spider asked. "If it's hidden, how we find it?"

"Because this package will have a smell," Ray said. "So you might smell it, though we can't. Our ability to smell isn't good enough. And we don't have dogs who can do this."

"Here's an example," said Jeff.

He held up a package of marijuana. It was packed like a brick with a cellophane wrapping.

"So you can smell it. See."

Jeff handed the package to Spider, and Spider put his nose to the package.

"Now hold it a little further away."

Spider did so, holding the package with his arm outstretched.

"Do you still smell something?" Jeff asked.

Spider nodded.

"Good," said Jeff. "That's what we want you to look for. In fact, there will be several dozen packages, so the smell should be even stronger."

Ray held up six backpacks and large black garbage bags. "When you find the packages, you can put them here. Afterwards bring the backpacks and bags to us. We'll take everything from there."

* * * * * * *

Excitedly, the Neanderthals piled into cars -- Scorpion, Spider, and Tarantula with Ray; Yellow Jacket, Wasp, and Hornet with Jeff, and they were on their way.

About an hour later, Ray and Jeff pulled into the parking lot on a small bluff overlooking the water. Below it was a beach, and a pathway of slats led to the water. On either side, boats were docked. Two security guards stood by the entrance, ready to check IDs to make sure only owners and their guests came to their boats.

Ray and Jeff led the way to the edge of the bluffs, and Ray pointed towards the boats.

"The packages are in the white boat that's second on the right side."

"How do you know?" said Scorpion.

"We got a tip," Ray said.

"We often get tips about such things," Jeff added. "We have friends around the area. They help us and we help them."

"That's nice," said Spider. "Friends."

"Now we wait and watch," said Ray. "We want to see who comes and goes, and we want to make sure no one is on the boat."

"We also have to figure out how to get past the guards," Jeff added.

For the next two hours, they all just watched. A few people stopped in front of the guards and pulled out wallets with IDs. Then, the guards shooed them on. But the people who entered went to other boats to check them. A few pulled up their boat's anchor and sailed away.

"That's a good sign," Ray commented to Jeff, as the Neanderthals standing around him listened. "No one's going to the boat we want to board."

"Maybe the boat owners are waiting for a pick-up when it gets dark. They're less likely to run into any other boaters that way," Jeff said.

Ray nodded. "Then, it would be good to send in our guys now."

"What about the guards?" Jeff asked. "It's harder to sneak by them in the day."

So what was the best approach? Ray and Jeff fell silent thinking, while the Neanderthals talked quietly among themselves about how to get on the boat and find what they were looking for.

Suddenly, Yellow Jacket stepped over to Ray and tapped him on the shoulder.

"We have an idea."

"Oh?" Ray looked around surprised.

"Yes. We all talked about it. Hornet, Wasp, and I can do something, so the guards look at us. Then, they chase us. And the others can go on the boat."

"Why that's genius," Ray said. "Yes. Do that."

He looked at the Neanderthals admiringly, though a little miffed at himself for not thinking of that idea.

"Yes, let's do it," Jeff said.

But as the Neanderthals filed down the bluff to the dock, Ray wondered if the idea would work. Could three Neanderthals distract the guards for long enough, so they wouldn't see the other three go on the boat? Would the boat owners stay away while the Neanderthals were there? And would any other owners who came to check their own boats see the Neanderthals and wonder why these strange-looking men were going onto a neighbor's boat.

Then, Ray stopped himself from asking the questions about why the plan to get the packages wouldn't work.

"Just think you can, and you can. Hope for the best and you are more likely to get it," he thought, echoing what the pastor at his church often said.

Then, he focused back on the Neanderthals as they walked down to the bottom of the bluff with their backpacks and bags. Once on the beach, they stood about 20 yards away from the guards at the entrance to the dock.

Would they make it? He felt he could only hope.

CHAPTER 25: THE BOAT

A few minutes later, the six gang members were on the beach.

"I can see the guards," Spider whispered.

"Yeah, they look tough," said Scorpion.

"Let's get them away," said Yellow Jacket.

"Be careful. They could shoot," warned Tarantula.

But the warning was too late. Yellow Jacket, Wasp, and Hornet were already running towards the dock.

Meanwhile, the guards, dressed in green security uniforms, were looking up and down the beach, which was mostly deserted, except for a few couples and families strolling along by the water or looking for shells.

Suddenly, Yellow Jacket put up his hand.

"Wait. Stop," he said. "We can't run straight at them. We have to confuse them."

He picked up one of the rounded stones from a dried out creek bed and threw it towards the guard. The rock landed a few feet away, and the guard turned to see what had just smashed to earth.

At the same time, Wasp and Hornet picked up rocks and threw them, so they landed several feet to the left and right of the first rock.

Now the guards looked around very confused.

"Let's go," said Yellow Jacket.

Whooping and hollering, Yellow Jacket, Wasp, and Hornet zigzagged quickly down the beach towards the guards. They each held a rock in each hand, and as they came closer, they threw the rocks, so they landed about two feet away from each guard.

Then, once the guards saw them, the three Neanderthals began running away -- Yellow Jacket to the right, Wasp and Hornet to the left, so the guards gave chase. One went after

Yellow Jacket, the other after Wasp and Hornet. The guards pulled out their guns to shoot, but Yellow Jacket, Wasp, and Hornet were still too far away so their shots went wild.

Soon the guards were huffing and puffing, while the Neanderthals found more rocks along the way and threw them, nearly hitting the guards and taunting them to keep following.

Meanwhile, with the guards on the beach far from the dock, Scorpion, Spider, and Tarantula ran quickly onto the dock with their backpacks and garbage bags for anything they found. Now if they could only find the boat and the packages.

As they looked for the boat, Yellow Jacket, Wasp, and Hornet kept on running until the guards were too far away to catch up or shoot. So the guards gave up the chase and returned to their post. Once again they stood ready to check the IDs of anyone trying to get onto the dock. But they didn't look behind them to see who was already on the dock. So Scorpion, Spider, and Tarantula relaxed. At least they were safe for now.

Soon they found the boat, a 25 foot sailboat, with the mainsail and headsail pulled down around the boom.

They glanced around to see if the dock was still clear.

"No one. Good," said Scorpion.

The three climbed onto the front deck that was moored to the dock.

Scorpion squatted down on his knees and motioned for the others to get down, too.

"We stay low. So no one sees us," said Scorpion.

"Now what?" asked Spider.

"We look for the packages."

He pointed to the steps leading to the cabin below.

"Let's go down," Scorpion suggested. "Maybe we find packages below."

Once at the bottom of the stairs, the Neanderthals saw the cabin spreading out in two directions with open doors that showed bunks and a storage area on one side, the kitchen and boiler room on the other, and a small bathroom between them.

Scorpion pointed to each area.

"Let's spread out," he said.

He motioned to Spider. "You take the kitchen area."

"Fine. I'm good at that," said Spider.

He motioned to Tarantula. "You take the bedroom and storeroom."

"Okay," Tarantula nodded.

Finally, Scorpion said, "I'll take the bathroom first. Then, I'll help each of you. Look and sniff around. If you find anything, let me know."

As Spider and Tarantula headed off, he had a last warning for them. "Don't throw things around. Don't make a mess. We don't want anyone to know we were here."

"Okay," Spider and Tarantula agreed.

The three headed off with their backpacks and garbage bags to search around the boat for anything they found.

For several minutes, Scorpion searched through the bathroom, opening every cabinet and holding his nose close to sniff for telltale signs of marijuana packages. He pulled open the frosted glass door to the shower, but nothing there either.

Meanwhile, Spider searched through the kitchen. He opened the cabinets above the sink, then dropped to his knees and looked under the sink. Next, he opened the door to the boiler room and squeezed into the narrow passageway between the boiler and the pipes running from it. As he looked carefully, he sniffed the air. Yet nothing smelled of marijuana.

At the same time, Tarantula searched through the bedroom. He carefully looked into each bunk, turned down the covers, and put them back in place. He sniffed at some of the bags and suitcases he found next to the beds. Yet they just smelled like the fabric of ordinary clothes, so there seemed no need to pry open the bags and suitcases.

After Scorpion found nothing, he returned to the entryway, as Spider came in from the kitchen.

"Nothing," said Spider. "I looked all over. There were so many smells from the food and spices. But I checked them all. Maybe there's nothing here."

"Maybe. But let's help Tarantula. He's not back yet."

So Scorpion and Spider headed into the bedroom, where Tarantula stood by the entrance to the storage area under the front deck.

"Nothing here so far," Tarantula told them. "But I still have to check the storage area."

"Then let's check it together," Scorpion said.

Tarantula went in first, as Scorpion and Spider stood by the entryway. It was a cramped area, filled with a jumble of suitcases and boxes. Tarantula had to squeeze between them and hunch over because of the low ceiling.

"It smells musty," Tarantula said. "Like nobody cleaned this area."

He sneezed from the dust. "It's really bad."

He pushed on ahead, and Scorpion followed him into the small space. He similarly bent over to avoid hitting the ceiling. Then, as he pressed into another aisle of boxes, he smelled it.

"There's something here," he announced.

He wriggled on, and found several boxes with Spanish writing.

"I think this is it," he said.

Scorpion pulled out his knife from its sheath on his belt and slithered it under the tape on top of the box. With a snap, the tops of the box fell open. Inside were several dozen of tightly wrapped packages of marijuana.

"We found it," Scorpion announced. "It's here."

Within minutes, he filled his backpack. Then, Spider handed him another and passed the filed backpack to Tarantula, like they were an assembly line.

About 20 minutes later, their backpacks were filed, and they had filled several large plastic garbage bags, too.

"Wow! This was easy," said Spider.

"Maybe. But we still have to get out and go to the cars," Scorpion said.

"Well, Ray and Jeff said the guards won't check us going out," Spider replied.

"Then, this should be easy," said Tarantula. "We take what we found and go."

"Okay," said Scorpion. "Everything's set."

They picked up their backpacks and hung them from their shoulders. Then, they grabbed their very full garbage bags. Spider and Tarantula lined up behind Scorpion, ready to follow him out.

But just as Scorpion was at the foot of the stairs, ready to climb onto the deck of the boat, the Neanderthals heard footsteps coming towards them on the dock.

"Oh, shit! We may have company soon," Scorpion said.

CHAPTER 26: THE RECKONING

The footsteps were coming closer. Closer.

Then, they were on the deck.

"Oh, no," whispered Scorpion. "They're on the boat."

"What can we do?" said Spider.

The three Neanderthals looked up towards the narrow opening with the stairs coming down into the small cabin area.

"They see us, we dead," Tarantula.

Now the footsteps stomped around the deck. Then, one set of footsteps headed to the front of the boat, while the other remained at the rear.

"Maybe only two people," Scorpion said. "If we can pass them, we can get out."

But how to pass them?

Scorpion started to ease gradually up the stairs to see if there was a way. Then, he pulled back, afraid to be seen.

He came back into the cabin area by the stairs.

"They can see us if we go out now."

Now the footsteps were coming towards the stairs.

"Wait. An idea," Spider suddenly said. "Maybe I, Tarantula take bags and hide in the storage room. You go into the kitchen. Make noise. They go there to check, and we run out."

Scorpion smiled.

"Let's try it. Nothing else to do."

As the footsteps came down the stairs, Spider and Tarantula headed into the storage room, their backpacks draped over their shoulders, and they each carried a large garbage bag. Meanwhile, Scorpion headed into the kitchen. He dropped off his backpack and bag in the boiler room and came back to the kitchen, closing the door to the boiler room behind him.

Moments later, two men, wearing jackets and slacks, appeared in the cabin.

"Let's get going," said one.

"I'll go to the cabin and release the anchor," said the other. "Then, we'll take everything to the CEO."

"And I'll check the count in each package to make sure we get paid the full amount."

"Good," the first man said, then started up the stairs.

But just as he reached the top, Scorpion dropped a pan in the kitchen.

The man on the stairs stopped, while the man in the cabin turned toward the sound.

"What the hell," he said. "Maybe someone's on the boat."

He turned and headed to the kitchen to check out the sound, while the man on the stairs came down to look. He pulled out his gun as he walked towards the kitchen. As he did, Scorpion stepped into the boiler room.

When Spider and Tarantula heard the men go into the kitchen, Spider pushed open the storage room door. He saw that the two men were no longer in the cabin.

"It's our chance," said Spider.

He ran into the cabin, still holding the garbage bag with the backpack hanging from his shoulder. Then, he headed toward the stairs. Tarantula, with a bag and backpack, followed right behind him.

Suddenly, with the weight of the two men on the stairs, the floorboards creaked.

In the kitchen, the two men heard the noise.

"Hey, what's that?" one man said.

"On the stairs," said the other.

They rushed there and saw Tarantula on the top step, as Spider clambered onto the dock.

"God damn!" the man with the gun exclaimed.

Then, he aimed and shot.

Tarantula felt the bullet hit his leg, and the pain spread out like a web. "Oh, no!" he gasped, unable to step up any further.

Spider looked back at Tarantula, feeling helpless to do anything to help, or he would get shot, too. So he turned and ran.

Just as the man with the gun came up to Tarantula, ready to shoot again, Tarantula dropped off the steps and into the water. Desperately, he clutched the bag, while his backpack floated behind him. The man shot again, but Tarantula swam under the dock. As the man climbed onto the dock to look for Tarantula, Spider ran down the dock to the beach.

At the same time, the second man emerged from the stairs and joined the first man on the deck.

The first man pointed at Spider and called out to his associate: "I'll go after him. You find this clown in the water."

As the first man chased after him, his gun out, Spider ran quickly, like a deer fleeing a hunter. From time to time he ducked down or zigzagged to the right or the left, so the shots whizzed by, just missing him by inches.

Then, Spider scrambled onto the beach. When the security guard looked towards the dock to see what the commotion was all about, Tarantula slipped by. Finally, on the roadway, he found the waiting cars with Ray and Jeff.

"Where's Scorpion and Tarantula?" Ray asked.

"You wait. They come," Spider said. "I hope," he added, as Ray and Jeff looked around nervously.

Minutes later, as the second man searched for Tarantula, Scorpion slowly climbed up the stairs to the beach with his backpack and bag. As he approached the top, he looked out. No one. So he inched up a little higher. Still no one.

Finally, he climbed out on the deck. In the distance he saw one man toward the end of the dock near the beach and the other man at the other end where other boats were lined up in their births.

So far so good. Quietly, Tarantula jumped from the boat onto the dock. Now, he thought, if he could manage to pass by the man near the beach, he might make it. So instead of running, he walked slowly, as if he was just another boat owner, enjoying the late afternoon. Occasionally, he stopped, put down his bag, and looked out over the water.

As the first man turned, giving up on finding Spider, Scorpion held his breath, hoping the man wouldn't realize who he was. For a few moments, the man looked around, then ran down the dock to help his associate find the man who jumped into the water.

Once the man was far down the dock, Scorpion resumed walking slowly like a tourist, so any sudden run wouldn't arouse suspicious if the man happened to look back.

Finally, Scorpion was on the beach, then past the security guard, and at last at the car. He was glad to see Spider had made it and was in the back seat.

"Where's Tarantula," Ray asked as Scorpion squeezed in beside Spider.

"He got shot. Jumped in water," Spider said. "I saw him jump. Now men try to find him."

"Oh, geez," said Ray. "We've got to help. You both stay here, and I'll tell Jeff. But first..." Ray got out of the car, and grabbed the backpacks and bags. "We'll lock up these."

After putting the backpacks and bags in the trunk, Ray went over to Jeff's car that was parked nearby in the parking lot.

"I'll get everything the guys got back safely. But now Tarantula is missing. He got shot and is in the water someplace, and the boat owners are looking for him."

"God damn," said Jeff. "If they find Tarantula with their stuff, and realize the other guys got away with their weed that could be bad. Real bad."

"Exactly. So you gotta find him before they do," Ray said. "God knows what they could do to him. Or maybe Tarantula could talk and give away everything."

"I'm on it," Jeff said, getting out of the car.

Then, as Jeff rushed towards the dock, Ray drove off with Spider and Scorpion. Ray was relieved that at least two of the guys had gotten back safely and their fat backpacks and bags showed they had made a major score against their rivals.

"Now if only Jeff can find Tarantula and help him get back," he thought. And if not? God, he didn't want to think about it.

Ray stepped on the gas, eager to get back to the warehouse as soon as he could.

CHAPTER 27: MAKING CHOICES

Jeff ran quickly toward the dock, hoping he was in time to save Tarantula.

Then, he came face to face with the security guard.

"Your ID and dock pass please," the guard said.

Jeff rummaged through his pockets looking for his wallet, and finally pulled it out. He decided to play the role of the busy businessman rather than pull out his gun to intimidate the guard, which might only lead the guard to call the cops, or worse, he might have to shoot the guard or get shot and killed himself.

Jeff handed over the wallet.

"Look, if you don't find my ID there, it's back in the office."

The guard began flipping through the cards in his wallet. Jeff acted increasingly irritated, hoping the guard wouldn't want to risk a messy confrontation.

"Look, I've got an important meeting," Jeff said. "I don't have time to go back for it."

The guard looked up. "Your pass isn't here."

"Okay. Okay. But I have to meet these people here for a big business deal."

"But I'm not supposed to let you through."

Jeff dug in his pocket and pulled out a $20 bill.

"Well, how about this? Will this let me through?"

The guard hesitated. Jeff pulled out another $20.

"Then how about this?"

Again, the guard hesitated.

"Okay. This is my last offer. Will you let me pass now?"

Jeff waved another $20 in front of the guard's face.

"Okay. Okay. Go. If it's that important to you."

"It is," said Jeff as he rushed in, relieved that he wouldn't have to threaten the guard with a gun or shoot him.

A minute later, Jeff was on the beach, running towards the dock. At first, he didn't see anyone ahead, as overhead clouds darkened the late afternoon sky.

Then, as he stepped onto the dock, he heard the rumble of voices in the distance. He couldn't make out the voices yet, but they seemed to be shouting.

He ran faster and faster, his hand grasping the handle of his gun just in case.

* * * * * *

Meanwhile, at the end of the dock, the two men found Tarantula. He was gasping for breath, as he held onto one post of the dock with one hand, while grasping the bag with the packages of marijuana in the other. His backpack still hung down from his neck, but now it was like an anchor pulling him down, as he struggled to stay above water.

One of the men pointed at him. "Look what he have here, George. Like a drowning rat."

"Yes, Niles. And it looks like he's holding onto something he took from us."

"So let's get him."

The two men lay down on the dock and reached out to Tarantula.

Niles grabbed his upper arm, while George pulled out his gun.

Tarantula tried to pull away, but he was weak from the loss of blood from the gunshot wound on his leg.

"So are you going to come out with us, or does my friend have to kill you?" Niles said.

Tarantula shook his head, as his grip on the post weakened.

"So what does that mean?" Niles said. "Are you coming with us?"

"Yes, yes," Tarantula gasped. "Don't kill."

Niles reached out his hand, and Tarantula grasped it. Niles then pulled him to the dock, as George stood up, bent over, and grabbed Tarantula's other hand, which was still holding onto the bag. Together, they pulled him onto the dock. Then, George opened the bag.

"Jesus!" he said. "He's got our packages of marijuana. Over a dozen of them."

Niles pulled off the backpack and opened it.

"My god! And here's another dozen or so packages."

He pushed Tarantula onto the dock so he lay cringing on his back. Then, noticing Tarantula's Neanderthal features for the first time, he looked at him, stunned.

"Who are you? What were you doing on our boat? How did you know about our shipment? Who sent you?"

Niles held up his fist, ready to strike.

"Please, no, no. I don't know. Just sent here."

"By who?" George screamed and grabbed Tarantula's neck. "You'll tell us or else." He began squeezing.

"No. No. Don't. Can't breathe," Tarantula gasped.

George released his hold. "Well, we want to keep you alive, don't we? We need you to talk. So talk."

"Don't know," Tarantula said again.

Niles struck him in the ribs with the butt of his gun.

"Oh, no," Niles said. "You have to know who sent you. So talk."

When Tarantula hesitated, thinking of what to say, Niles hit him again and again.

"No! No! Please," Tarantula screamed, writhing in agony.

George saw his bleeding leg and hit him there.

Tarantula groaned. He tried to reach out with his hands to protect his ribs and legs, but George and Niles hit him again and again.

"Okay. Please no. Two men sent us."

George and Niles paused their beating.

"Two men," George said. "What two men?"

"And who is us?" Niles asked. "What us? Who else was involved in this?"

George slapped Tarantula across the face. "So tell us now. What two men and who were you with?"

Then, Niles looked more closely at Tarantula's face and screamed out. "And your face. Why do you look like you do? Were you a fighter? Did someone mess up your face?"

He slapped Tarantula hard across the face again. "Yeah, tell us everything now, or we'll mess up your face even more."

But before Tarantula could answer or George or Niles could hit him again, a bullet whizzed by nearly hitting George in the head.

George and Niles turned around, their guns drawn.

Jeff shot again, but missed. He ducked as George and Niles shot back.

Once more, Jeff shot, this time, grazing Niles' shoulder.

"Shit!" Niles cried out.

He grabbed his bleeding shoulder, and when he tried to raise his arm to shoot again, he couldn't lift it

"Damn!" he cried out. "I'm done!"

He sat down nursing his shoulder, while George continued shooting at Jeff.

But the shots whizzed past his head, and Jeff ducked into one of the boats at the docks. He hid out for a few minutes, as George looked around, wondering where Jeff went. Then, when George turned back towards Tarantula, who had pulled himself up into a sitting position, another shot from Jeff whizzed by.

George ducked behind Tarantula to shield himself, and was about to shoot, when Jeff shot again from the boat, grazing his arm. George clenched his teeth through the pain, and got ready to shoot again.

Then he heard sirens.

"Damn!" he called out to Niles, who was hunched over near Tarantula and nursing his wounded shoulder. "The cops! Someone must have reported the shooting. Let's get out of here."

He grabbed the bag and backpack.

"But how do we get out of here? The cops are coming," said George. "And what if they see us with all this weed?"

"Curtains," said Niles.

"Then, what if we get back to our boat and stash it there," George suggested.

But there was no time to get there, since six cops were now running across the beach and nearing the dock, their guns drawn.

"No way now," said Niles. "They'll see us. This is the only way."

Holding the bag and backpack, Niles jumped into the water.

"Let's swim for it," he called back to George. "We can make it to the nearby beach. Then, get to our cars from there."

George jumped in to join him, and they swam off.

From the boat he had jumped into, Jeff saw Niles and George leap into the water, and he quickly ran over to Tarantula.

"Are you okay?" he said.

"Yeah, I think so," Tarantula replied. "But I hurt pretty bad."

"Well, we'll fix you up. Come on. Get up. Act like you're just a boat owner and nothing is wrong."

"Okay," said Tarantula.

He staggered up, leaning on Jeff for support.

Jeff saw the six cops stepping on to the dock, but he didn't want to try passing them. Not with a wounded Neanderthal. Though Tarantula didn't have any drugs on him, there would be questions. Why did he look as he did? Why was he black and blue and bleeding? Why were his clothes all wet? Then, that might lead to more questions, maybe a police report, and a search for suspects. And certainly they would want to see their IDs. So no, not that.

Jeff thought quickly, then noticed that the boat next to them was unoccupied.

"Let's go here," he said, and in moments, he and Tarantula were on the boat.

As the cops came near, looking around for anyone suspicious on the dock, Jeff noticed some deck chairs.

"Let's sit down like we're talking," he told Tarantula. "We don't want to suddenly walk away from them or go down into the cabin, since that might look suspicious."

So when the police officers came by, Jeff and Tarantula were facing each other in two chairs, apparently engaged in conversation.

"Did you see anyone shooting?" one officer asked.

"No nothing," said Niles. "We just heard some shots, but saw nothing."

"Okay," said the officer. He reached over and handed Jeff a business card. "Feel free to call me if you learn anything from anyone. The guard said there were dozens of shots here about ten minutes ago."

"Sure thing," said Jeff, pocketing the card. As the cops moved on along the dock, he sunk back into the chair relieved,

"Now we wait," he said to Tarantula. "As soon as they are gone, we can go."

About 20 minutes later, it was all clear. The cops were gone. Jeff helped Tarantula out of the boat, and as Tarantula leaned against him, they walked down the dock to the beach.

When they approached the security guard, Jeff told him, "My friend's sick. I'm taking him to a doctor."

The guard quickly waved them on.

A few minutes later they were at Jeff's car. Tarantula crawled into the back and lay down. Seconds later, they were on their way back to headquarters. .

"At least you were able to get several bags of the stuff," Jeff told Tarantula. "We got you back safe, and we'll have you fixed up in no time. So don't feel bad."

Tarantula nodded. "Thanks."

A few minutes later he was sleep, as Jeff drove on, glad that the operation had been mostly a success, except for the boat owners coming back too soon. At least, the team came away with several dozen packages of marijuana that could be worth millions on the street. Plus the operation proved that the Neanderthal team could help them conduct these operations. They just had to have a better plan for the next time.

CHAPTER 28: COLLECTING WHAT'S DUE

A few days after the Neanderthals' operation at the docks, Ray called them into his office. He sat at his desk, Jeff beside him. Several piles of marijuana bundles were spread across the desk.

As the six team members sat down across from him, Tarantula held up his arm.

"I'm almost healed now," Tarantula said. "See. I can move everything like always. Pain almost gone."

"Good. So you can join our next operation. And that's what I want to tell you about today."

Ray pointed to the marijuana bundles on his desk.

"You see! That's what you guys got. So the operation was a success. I know it went a little haywire at the end. And I'm sorry you got beat up, Tarantula. But you guys still got a major haul, and you didn't get caught by the cops. So you're a great team. And this is program really working. Just like we hoped."

Ray raised his hand with the high-five sign and smiled broadly.

"So congratulate yourselves. You deserve it."

The Neanderthals smiled at each other and similarly raised the high-five sign to each other.

"Very good," said Ray. "And by way of thanks, here are some treats just for you."

Ray opened a jar of honey and bag of crackers. He reached down and pulled up a half-dozen more jars and bags.

"One is for each of you. So thanks again."

Ray passed around the honey and crackers and then held up a large photo of a street with small retail shops -- a clothing store, liquor store, hair stylist, jewelry store, and others.

"Okay. This is your next assignment," Ray said. "You're going to collect money from people in most of these shops. We'll give you cards with the picture of each store and how much to collect from the owner. You just have to give the shop owner the card, and they will give you money."

"Why we do this?" Scorpion asked. "Why they give us money?"

"It's for protection," Ray said.

"Yeah," Jeff added. "We help the store owners, so they pay us for our help."

"Okay," Scorpion nodded. "So we help you get the money?"

"Yes, exactly," said Ray.

He smiled at Jeff, pleased that the Neanderthals, or at least Scorpion so far, seemed to understand what to do.

Ray explained a few more details about how they would go in, two to a store.

"And Jeff and I will be waiting for you in two cars down the street, so when you're done, we'll take you home. Then, you can do this every month, along with some other operations we have planned for you."

The meeting over, the Neanderthals returned to their cabin, where they talked happily among themselves, while enjoying their honey and crackers.

* * * * * * *

The next day, the operation, which Ray dubbed, "Operation Protection" began. Ray with Scorpion, Spider, and Tarantula in one car, and Jeff with Yellow Jacket, Hornet, and Wasp in the other, drove to one end of the street with the retail shops and parked.

They all gathered in a small group on the corner, and Ray handed each of the Neanderthals a satchel that looked like a shopping bag with an over-the-shoulder strap. Then, he held up a packet of cards.

"These cards show the stores to go to and the amount of money to collect," he explained. "There's a picture and name of each store on each card. Ask for the store owner. Then, tell the owner or assistant at the counter that Ray and Jeff sent you. Say you are there to collect the money for them. The owner or assistant will know what to do."

Ray paused, while the Neanderthals glanced at the cards.

"You understand," he asked.

The Neanderthals nodded, and he continued.

"They will give you the money, and you will put it in the satchel. You will also fold the card for that store around the money you get. And that's it."

The Neanderthals looked around at the shops along either side of the street, then back at Ray.

"You'll go in groups of three," Ray added. "Scorpion, Spider, and Tarantula, you take the stores to the left as you go down the street. Yellow Jacket, Hornet, and Wasp, you take the stores on the right."

The Neanderthals nodded.

"So you understand?"

"Yes, get money. Put it in the bag," said Scorpion,

"Right," said Ray.

"And you say you were sent by Ray and Jeff."

"Okay," said Scorpion. "We do that."

"What if they say no money?" Spider asked.

Ray looked at Jeff uncertainly, since he was used to getting their money each month, no questions. He turned back to the Neanderthals.

"If they say no money, tell them we will talk to them."

"Then, they will probably give you the money," said Jeff

"But if they don't, tell them to talk to us," Ray said.

As the Neanderthals set off down the street, Ray and Jeff watched them go, beaming proudly, like parents who just sent their children off to their first day of school.

"You see. I told you it would work," Ray commented to Jeff.

"Yeah," said Jeff.

"And we don't have to worry about them stealing from us, like the other guys we used for collectors. They don't understand the value of money and what it can buy."

"At least not yet," Jeff said.

"And not ever, let's hope," said Ray.

"But they look a lot different than the other guys we've used," Jeff asked. "Could that be a problem?"

"Nah," Ray replied. "The retailers they're contacting know us. They know the score. They'll probably think the Neanderthals are boxers or wrestlers, or something like that. And with three of our guys together, sure, they'll pay up. What could go wrong?"

Ray looked down the street and grinned, feeling a surge of pride and confidence. He was glad to see that the Neanderthals were already heading toward the stores.

* * * * * * *

At first Scorpion, Spider, and Tarantula were a little unsure of what they were doing. So they walked in slowly to the first store along the street, a clothing boutique. Once inside, they took a few minutes to walk around like regular customers to get up their courage.

Scorpion loved touching the fabric of the suits on the manikins. It felt so soft to the touch as he stroked it. Meanwhile, Spider tried on some hats on a rack near the mirror and grinned at his reflection.

"It looks good," he said, to Tarantula, who stood nearby.

Then, Tarantula began fingering the bracelets and necklaces in a bowl above a glass counter that held several rows of watches. He noticed that the rows of watches moved around as the display rotated. "Fascinating" he thought, as he watched like a cat seeing its prey move back and forth, while it decided the best time to pounce.

Just then, the saleswoman, a tall woman in a sleek black dress and long blonde hair, came over to him

"Can I help you find something?" she said.

Tarantula jerked up with a start, and Scorpion and Spider came over to him.

"Is there something you are looking for? I can help," the saleswoman said.

"Oh, no. We just look," said Scorpion. "We come to speak to your owner."

"Oh, okay," the saleswoman said, surprised. "I'll bring him to you."

A few minutes later, the owner, a 40something man with short graying hair, glasses, and a light brown suit, came out from the back of the store.

"What do you want to see me about?" the owner said.

Scorpion handed him the card with the picture of his shop and the number 200 written on it.

The owner looked at the card, then back at Scorpion.

"We are from Ray and Jeff," Scorpion said. "He sent us."

"He said you know what to do," Spider added.

The owner nodded. "Yes. Okay."

He pulled out a cashbox and took out two $100 bills. He handed them to Scorpion.

"I understand, and I don't want to mess with them. But you look so different from the other guys."

"We're new," said Scorpion.

"We just started," said Spider.

"Thank you very much," said Tarantula.

Then, as Ray had instructed, Scorpion folded the card with the store picture over the $200 and put it in the satchel.

"That was easy," Scorpion said to Spider and Tarantula as they walked out. "Now we go to all the stores on the cards. We do what Ray and Jeff said.

Meanwhile, on the other side of the street, Yellow Jacket, Hornet, and Wasp were similarly going into the stores. Similarly, they held out their cards with the amount of money to collect from a store, and placed the card and money together in their satchel.

For the next hour, the two teams went in and out of stores collecting money, as Ray and Jeff sat in their cars waiting for them to return. Ray peered out with his binoculars, then called Jeff on his phone.

"It's going so well," said Ray, as he watched Scorpion, Spider, and Tarantula come out of a fashion boutique.

"I know," Jeff agreed, looking through his set of binoculars. "And Yellow Jacket, Hornet, and Wasp appear to be doing fine. It's great how the merchants have accepted paying them this way."

"And that's because they know us. They're willing to pay, because they know what we'll do to them if they don't."

"Exactly," Jeff agreed.

He raised his binoculars to his eyes and resumed watching, and Ray did the same.

CHAPTER 29: CAN I HAVE IT?

About an hour later, Scorpion, Spider, and Tarantula finished contacting all of the shops on their cards.

"We're done," Scorpion said. "We did it. Ray will be very happy."

"And everyone was so nice," Spider said. "We just said we were there for Ray and Jeff. They knew who they were. Then, they gave us what it said on the card."

They headed back, and when they saw Ray standing by his car, they waved eagerly.

"We spoke to everyone," Scorpion yelled.

"Wonderful," Ray called out, and he happily waved back.

Meanwhile, on the other side of the street, Yellow Jacket, Hornet, and Wasp were finishing up. Then, Wasp noticed a jewelry store at the end of the street.

"Wait," he said, as Yellow Jacket and Hornet turned, ready to head back to the car.

Wasp moved close to the store window and glanced at the shiny gold necklaces and bracelets which had different arrangements of rubies, pearls, sapphires, jades, and other stones.

"Come look," he said, motioning for Yellow Jacket and Hornet to join him at the window.

Soon the three of them were gazing at the gems.

"They're beautiful," Wasp said. "I like them a lot."

"Me, too," said Hornet.

"But the store isn't on our cards," Yellow Jacket said.

"I know. Maybe Ray and Jeff forgot," Wasp suggested. "We went to all the other stores on the street."

"That's so," Hornet agreed.

"Now we have to go. We're done," Yellow Jacket said, and turned to leave.

Still Wasp insisted, "But the jewelry is so nice. Let's go in."

"Okay," Yellow Jacket finally agreed.

He followed Wasp and Hornet into the store.

The storekeeper at the counter, a woman in her 30s wearing a flowered blouse, looked at them warily. They looked so different from the customers who usually came into the store. They appeared very husky and strong, like wrestlers; and their T-shirts and jeans set them apart, too. No, they were not the usual buyers of luxury jewelry. They were usually women in their 30s or older, who came dressed in pant suits or tailored dresses; and sometimes they were accompanied by their boyfriends or husbands, who came wearing sports jackets and slacks or dark power suits and ties.

"Can I help you?" the store keeper said nervously.

Wasp came over to the counter holding a gold brooch shaped like a butterfly, with jade eyes and ruby wings. Yellow Jacket and Hornet followed and stood beside him, Yellow Jacket to his left, Hornet to his right.

"Very nice," Wasp said. He pointed to the woman's blouse with colorful daisies and lilacs. "Very nice, too."

The storekeeper blushed self-consciously. "Uhmm, thank you. But how can I help you. What do you want?"

Wasp held out the brooch. "Can I have this?" he said.

"Uhhh, it's five thousand," the store keeper said.

"Five thousand? What do you mean?" said Wasp.

The storekeeper shifted awkwardly from one foot to the other. She glanced from Wasp to the two men on either side, unsure what to say, and growing very scared.

"Five thousand dollars," she said finally. "That's what it costs."

"I don't understand. Ray and Jeff sent us," Wasp said.

"Who's Ray and Jeff?" the storekeeper said.

"They know everyone," Yellow Jacket replied. "We work for them."

"Yes," Hornet said. "They're very nice. So we help them."

"And I like this pin a lot. A butterfly. Can I have it?"

"But it's five thousand. Five thousand," the storekeeper gulped. "Do you have that? You need that amount to get this."

Wasp hesitated for a few moments, not fully understanding what the storekeeper wanted. With the other storekeepers the meeting had gone so smoothly. Give them a card. Say they were there for Ray and Jeff. Then get some money, put it in a bag, and go. But now this woman asked all these odd questions.

"We can ask Ray and Jeff," Wasp said finally. "We can..."

But before he could finish, the storekeeper's husband came out and stormed over to them.

"What's going on?" he said angrily. "What do you guys want?"

He glared at Wasp and then at Yellow Jacket and Hornet.

Wasp became very nervous. He held up the gold butterfly brooch with the jade eyes and ruby wings.

"I just want this," he said. "We're here from Ray and Jeff. They can tell you..."

"Tell me what?" the husband yelled.

From under the counter, he pulled out a gun and pointed it at Wasp.

"Now you all get out. Get out!"

"Please, no. You don't understand," said Wasp.

"Oh, I understand very well. You want to steal this. Now out."

Wasp, Yellow Jacket, and Hornet stepped back. Wasp grasped the gold brooch even more tightly.

"No. Please listen," Wasp begged.

But the husband yelled back: "No, you go now. Out. Get Out."

He waved the gun in the air. "I mean it. Get out."

"Please, wait," Wasp pleaded.

"Just go, or I'll shoot."

"And put down the pin," the woman storekeeper called out.

But it was too late. Still holding the brooch, Wasp turned and raced towards the door, Yellow Jacket and Hornet right behind him.

The husband aimed. Blam, the gun went off. But the shot went wild, as Wasp, Yellow Jacket, and Hornet rushed out the door.

The husband shot again, but last shot only grazed Hornet's belt. Moments later, they were out on the street, running as fast as they could to Jeff's car.

Meanwhile, the husband called 911.

"Hello, police. I want to report a robbery. By three men who looked like wrestlers."

"What did they take?" the dispatcher wanted to know.

"A $5000 brooch. A butterfly with jade stones and rubies."

"We'll be right there," she said.

"They're running away now," the husband said. "They're going down the street."

But by the time two police cars arrived with sirens blaring and four officers came into the store, Wasp, Yellow Jacket, and Hornet had hopped into Jeff's car, and he roared off.

"We didn't see anyone matching your description on the street," one officer told the storekeeper and her husband.

"But there's a video," the husband replied.

He pointed to the two cameras on the ceiling, which took running videos of what was happening in the store from two angles.

"Maybe that will help us," said the officer.

So the husband climbed up on a stool to reach each camera and pulled out the video reel. He handed the reels over to the officer.

"We'll look at it when we get back to the station," the offer said.

Then, another officer pulled out a clipboard and began asking questions about the incident for the report. What happened? What were the three men like? What did they wear? What did they say? What did they take? How much was it worth?

The questions went on and on. Finally, officer with the clipboard said they had all the information they needed.

"We'll let you know what we find out," he said.

"Thanks, officer," the husband said. "I hope you find those damn bastards. And they've got to be gang members. They kept talking about their leaders, Ray and Jeff."

CHAPTER 30: WHAT'S NEXT?

Back in Ray's office, the six Neanderthals sat across from Ray, while Jeff sat beside him, taking notes.

"Well, we did it," said Scorpion, passing the bag with the cards and money to Ray.

He glanced through it quickly to check that all the collected money was there.

"We got the money from everyone," Scorpion continued. "Everyone said they knew you, and they gave us money. What it said on the card."

"That's great," said Ray. "And it looks like it's all here."

He turned to Jeff. "Write down what we collected and from who."

Ray turned back to the Neanderthals. "You did well. I knew you could do it. So that will be one of your jobs now. Every week you can go to the same stores and collect more money, just like you did today."

Scorpion, Spider, and Tarantula smiled happily. They shook hands and patted each other on the back.

Ray turned to Yellow Jacket, Hornet, and Wasp.

"We have a problem," he announced.

"But we saw everyone you said to see," said Yellow Jacket, as he handed Ray the bag with the cards and money. "There. You see."

Ray glanced through the bag and pulled out each card with the money attached.

"Yes, I see that. And that's fine. But afterwards you went into another store."

"We only went in to see the jewelry," Yellow Jacket said.

"It was so pretty," said Wasp.

"But that's the problem," Ray said. "That was…"

Yellow Jacket interrupted. "We tried to tell the man and woman in the store. Wasp wanted to know how to get it."

"So I said they could ask you," Wasp said. "You and Jeff."

"Ask us?" Ray said. "And did you give them our names?"

"Oh, yes. Like we did with everyone," Wasp said.

"Oh, Christ!" Ray gasped. He was fuming now, ready to explode. He gripped the edges of his desk to hold himself back. "So you told them our names?"

"Yes. Like you said to do."

"But that was only in the stores we told you to enter. And now..."

Ray turned to Jeff. "We have a really serious problem. Not only did the owners chase the guys out of the store, but they probably got what happened on camera, if they have video surveillance in their store. And even if they don't, they have our names."

"But we got away," said Hornet. "When the cops came, we got in Jeff's car. He drove away."

"Yes, but the cops can investigate. They can check the license plate number."

"We can change that," Jeff said.

"Yes," Ray agreed. "But the cops still have our names. And if the owners have cameras, they will show their faces. And even if they don't, the store owners will still recognize them."

"Oh," said Yellow Jacket.

"I just wanted to ask them about the pretty pin," Wasp said.

"Then, the man pulled out a gun," said Hornet. "He shot at us."

"That doesn't matter," Ray said. "They saw the three of you and got scared. They thought you came there to rob them."

"No, no," Wasp protested.

"That's why they called 911, the emergency police call line. And that's why the cops came."

"But we got away," Yellow Jacket protested.

"That doesn't matter, if they investigate and find us," Ray said.

"At least you didn't take anything," Jeff commented. "So we can explain it's just a misunderstanding."

"That's true. We can do that," Ray agreed.

"But I did take the pin," Wasp said.

He pulled out the butterfly brooch with the green jade eyes and red ruby wings. He laid it on the desk in front of Ray.

"See. It's so pretty. Then, when the man shot his gun, we just run. We run very fast. And I was holding the pin. So I kept holding it when we ran."

"What!" Ray gasped. "You had this."

"I didn't want to drop it," Wasp continued. "I thought you can get it for me. Or you can return it. But I really like it. I would like to keep it."

Ray looked at Jeff in terror, his face white with fear.

"Now we have an even bigger problem. The Neanderthals don't understand how serious this is. What should we do?"

Jeff began shaking himself. He pursed his lips tightly together. "I don't know," he said. "I just don't know."

CHAPTER 31: WE'VE GOT A PROBLEM, TOO

"I want to show you a video," Lt. Davis began, as he sat in his office across from the six Neanderthals Force members, Adam, Brad, Charlie, Derrick, Eddy, and Fred. Beside him were Sgt. Burrows and Sgt. Garrett.

"I saw this in our department briefing today, and this concerns all of us. We have to do something about it."

Lt. Davis played the video on the ceiling monitor. It showed the three Neanderthals -- Yellow Jacket, Hornet, and Wasp -- walking into the jewelry store. Then, Wasp picked up the butterfly brooch and took it over to the counter.

"Now watch. It gets messy," Lt. Davis said.

As everyone watched, the video showed Wasp holding the brooch, as he, along with Yellow Jacket and Hornet, talked to the storekeeper. Then, her husband came out with a gun and chased the three Neanderthals away."

Lt. Davis continued. "Though the three ran off, as you can see, the owners called this in as a robbery, and it was, because one of the robbers left with the pin. So it's not just an attempted robbery."

Lt. Davis clicked a button and stopped the video.

"At least, the cops have some leads. The names Ray and Jeff. The license plate of the black Chevy, their get-away car, though they might quickly change the plate. But we still have a description of the car. And the robbers took a $5000 piece of jewelry, so if they try to pawn it, they're cooked. Every pawn shop in the area will be on the alert."

"So why are we seeing this?" Sgt. Burrows asked. "Won't the property crimes division handle this like any other robbery?"

"Yes, they will. But what's important for us is who the robbers are. Look at the video again."

With a few more clicks, Lt. Davis restarted the video from the beginning.

"Now look closely," he said, and the video began to play.

When the three men came over to the counter and one held up the brooch, the camera showed their unmasked faces.

"They're Neanderthals!" Adam called out.

"Yes, they are," Brad agreed.

"That's exactly right," Lt. Davis said. "And that's the problem. We thought you guys were the only Neanderthals out there, our secret squad going after hard to catch criminals. But now...."

Lt. Davis paused, trying to decide how to best explain the significance of this revelation for the team.

"Well, let me put it this way. What this video means is that there is another team of Neanderthals out there. The video only shows three. But there could be more. Many more. We don't know.

"But what we do know, is that someone else is bringing back Neanderthals and they're not just training them to work and become part of a workforce. Instead, they're turning them into criminals. It's like they've created a new criminal gang, and God knows how big it is. It could be huge, really huge. Who knows?"

"Wow!" said Charlie.

"We didn't know," said Derrick.

"Yeah. So there you have it," said Lt. Davis. "We can't only go out to find and catch criminals when other cops can't bring them in. We've got to go after this gang, too. We've got to find out who's in charge of these guys in the gang. And we've got to put the whole gang and their handlers out of business."

"What if they help the criminals we're trying to catch?" Adam asked.

"Yeah, that, too," Lt. Davis said.

"And what if they come after us?" Fred wondered. "I mean if they're Neanderthals, they might fight us, too."

"I hadn't thought of that," said Lt. Davis. "But any and all things are possible. God knows what they might try to do."

Lt. Davis turned to Sgt. Burrows and Sgt. Garrett.

"This video could be the tip of the iceberg. I mean, we could be up again a big and growing Neanderthal gang or gangs being led by some savvy human gang leaders. So just like we got some Neanderthals from a robot factory owner and trained them, these gang leaders must be working with their own team of scientists and trainers. I'm sure this is just the beginning of something that could become really big."

"That sounds terrible," Sgt. Burrows commented.

"Yes, it," Lt. Davis continued. "And worse, these Neanderthal gangsters might not just commit crimes against everyday citizens, but they could help other criminals and attack us. So we've got to do something to stop this gang now. We've got to track them down and arrest them and whoever is leading them."

"How do we do that?" Sgt. Garrett asked.

"How?" Lt. Davis pondered. "I'm not sure right now. But we've got to start investigating. And beyond that, I just don't know."

ABOUT THE AUTHOR

GINI GRAHAM SCOTT, Ph.D., J.D., is a nationally known writer, consultant, speaker, and seminar leader, specializing in business and work relationships, professional and personal development, social trends, popular culture, science, and crime. She has published over 50 books with major publishers. She has worked with dozens of clients on self-help, popular business books, memoirs, and film scripts.

She is the founder of Changemakers Publishing, featuring books on work, business, psychology, self-help, and social trends. The company has published over 150 print and e-books and over 100 audiobooks. She has licensed several dozen books for foreign sales, including the UK, Russia, Korea, Spain, and Japan.

She has received national media exposure for her books, including appearances on *Good Morning America, Oprah,* and *CNN.* She has been the producer and host of a talk show series, *Changemakers,* featuring interviews on social trends.

She brings to *The Return of the Neanderthals* a special interest in current social trends and new developments in science and technology. Her books in this area include:

The Science of Living Longer: Developments in Life Extension Technology (Praeger) (also turned into a documentary: *The New Age of Aging,* released in June 2019)

The Very Next New Thing: (Praeger)

Back to the Middle Ages (AKA: The New Middle Ages - Nortia Press)

Lies and Liars: How and Why Sociopaths Lie (Skyhorse Publishing)

Scammed: Learn from the Biggest Consumer and Money Frauds (Allworth Press).

She also brings her considerable skills as a scriptwriter and executive producer of nine features, documentaries, and TV pilots, which are in distribution, release, or post production through joint ventures with Changemakers Productions. The most recently released include *Driver; The New Age of Aging; Deadly Infidelity; Me, My Dog, and I; Rescue Me; Courage to Continue;* and *Reversal.*

She has developed stories in writing memoirs for clients. Among those which have been published are:

At Death's Door with Sebastian Sepulveda (Rowman & Littlefield) (also turned into a TV pilot *Death's Door*)

From School to War: Growing Up in Hitler's Germany by Wolf Dettbarn (Truman State)

American Justice? with Paul Brakke (TouchPoint Press) (the first of 9 books from American Leadership Books)

She brings to the book an extensive experience in marketing, sales, and promotion,. Additionally, she does workshops and writes books about writing and self-publishing to help other writers publish their books. These books include:

Increase Your Impact and Influence '
How to Find and Work with a Good Ghostwriter
Self-Publishing Secrets
Self-Publishing Your Book in Multiple Formats
Make More Money with Your Book
Conducting a Monthly Social Media Video Campaign

Scott is active in a number of community and business groups, including the Lafayette, Pleasant Hill, and Walnut Creek Chambers of Commerce. She is a graduate of the prestigious Leadership Contra Costa program and the member of several business networking groups. She does workshops and seminars on the topics of her books and on self-publishing.

She received her Ph.D. from the University of California, Berkeley, and her J.D. from the University of San Francisco Law School. She has received five MAs at Cal State University, East Bay, including in Popular Culture and Lifestyles and Communication.

CHANGEMAKERS PUBLISHING

3527 Mt. Diablo Blvd., #273

Lafayette, CA 94549

changemakers@pacbell.net . (925) 385-0608

www.changemakerspublishingandwriting.com

www.ingramcontent.com/pod-product-compliance
Lightning Source LLC
Chambersburg PA
CBHW070956190726
48292CB00004B/1476